Enjoy Balance and Unleash Creativity

Five Steps to
a Happier, Healthier and
Successful Life

Madan Birla
with Cecelia Miller Marshall, Ph.D.

VISHWAKARMA PUBLICATIONS VP®

Enjoy Balance and Unleash Creativity
Five Steps to a Happier, Healthier and Successful Life

1st Edition - Published by Vishwakarma Publications in December 2016

© Madan Birla

ISBN - 978-93-85665-55-4

Published by:
Vishwakarma Publications
283, Budhawar Peth, Near City Post, Pune- 411 002.
Phone No: (020) 20261157 Email: info@vpindia.co.in
Website: www.vpindia.co.in

Cover Design
Rahul Dhamane

Typeset and Layout
Gold Fish Graphics, Pune.

Printed at
Repro India Pvt. Ltd., Mumbai

₹ 300/-

To Shashi, Naveen, Nita,
Kunal and Manisha who make my
life journey fun and fulfilling

Acknowledgements

First, I want to thank Vishal Soni at Vishwakarma Publications for his interest, encouragement and excellent support. Geeta Hosmane at the Mahratta Chamber of Commerce, Industries and Agriculture, and Preeti Gupta at Aditya Birla group HQ, deserve special thanks for organizing the Balance workshops in Pune and Mumbai respectively.

The workshops and conversations at Tata Consultancy Services (TCS), Noida, and Microsoft, Bengaluru helped me greatly in educating myself about the unique work-life balance challenges faced by professionals and managers in India.

I really appreciate Achint Choudhry's help in not just reviewing and editing the chapters, but also making suggestions to improve the contents. I want to convey my sincere thanks to Karen Anand, Ravi Talwar, Gaurav Mathur, and Vandana Saxena Poria for making time in their busy schedules to meet and answer my questions.

Finally, I want to convey my deepest appreciation to Shashi, my life partner, for teaching me to enjoy the simple pleasures of life and keeping me balanced.

Content

Content

Chapter 1

What Started Me on My Balance Journey?

One day I found myself standing in my physician's office saying, "Lately I have not been as effective at work as I used to be, especially in dealing with people. I am not listening well and find myself upset over things of little or no consequence. And physically, I feel drained when I get home."

He told me it was all normal, considering my increasing responsibilities at work, but prescribed some tranquilizers anyway. On the drive home, however, I kept telling myself that I was not going to get dependent on tranquilizers. I just don't like putting chemicals in my body.

He had me undergo a thorough physical, which indicated that I had a "pre-ulcer condition." He asked me to stay away from spicy foods. I said, "Doc, you don't understand! I'm an Indian and asking me to stop eating spicy food is like saying, 'Don't breathe!'"

So I began extensive research into the root cause of my emotional and physical distress. Seemingly, I should have been on top of the world. In 10 years at RCA, I had earned three promotions and moved into management. I owned a fine home in a nice suburb with a big yard and two cars in the driveway. I had achieved affluence and success, and had a loving wife and two healthy children.

Over time, however, it became clear to me that the primary cause for the symptoms of stress I was experiencing was that I was trying to do more and more in less and less time. As a result, my life was out of balance. At an ever-increasing cost to my personal life, work was consuming most of my time and energy. In addition to the full time job I was also working on my MBA at nights.

After moving to Memphis to join Federal Express, I continued my search for solutions to balanced-life issues. This research led me to complete a master's degree in counseling. After presenting a paper called Managerial Productivity and Life Balance at the American Counseling Association's annual conference, I sent a copy to Mr. Frederick Smith, Founder, Chairman and Chief Executive Officer of Federal Express.

I received a call from his office that a meeting has been set up to discuss the paper. It was a day before the Thanksgiving holiday and Fred was in a relaxed mood. After a good exchange, Fred suggested I develop and teach a seminar based on the paper for Federal Express managers. For six years I conducted the two-day 'Leadership and Balanced Life' seminar at Federal Express.

Rhodes College called me and said that they'd like to offer this class to other executives in town. Cecilia Miller Marshall and her husband attended one of my workshops at Rhodes. She is a psychologist in her own Marriage and Family practice. After the class, Cecilia said, "Madan, most of the people I see in my practice do not really have any deep psychological issues. Their dual careers and other demands create stress leading to relationship problems. I'm interested in this subject, and if you want to write articles I'll be happy to collaborate with you."

We started with an article, and before we knew it we had ten chapters for a book! The American edition of the book was based on the concepts from my seminar and personal interviews conducted in the U.S.

Knowing his interest in the subject, I sent a copy of the manuscript to Fred and received an encouraging note that read

-

Madan,

Thank you for sending this. Could not read it all, but selected readings herein convinced me that you are very perceptive of the human race's foibles and aspirations.

Best,

Fred (Founder & CEO, FedEx)

Dr. Cecilia Miller Marshall's participation

I chose to participate in this project, not because I have achieved the perfect balance in my life, but because I believe the quest is so important. In my personal and professional experiences, I see balanced-life concerns everywhere.

Many families who seek therapy are not suffering deeply rooted psychological problems. They are simply suffering from the physical and emotional exhaustion that comes from trying to do too many things at once.

I am grateful to friends, family, clients and colleagues who have shared with me their own quests for a balanced life. Whenever the experiences of others are reported in this book, all details and identifying information have been significantly altered in order to preserve privacy and confidentiality. Any resemblance of the stories to actual individuals is purely coincidental. It is quite likely, however, that the stories you read will sound quite familiar — because the search for a satisfying life is something we all have in common!

'The Genesis of Balanced Life' Book's Indian Edition

Several years ago I was invited by Microsoft, Bangalore to conduct a 'Balanced Life' workshop. Management's concern was that after 3-4 years on the job their higher-level engineers and managers were burning out. During my yearly India visits I started noticing work-life balance concerns.

Burnout Blues Hit Young Indian IT Pros *(Economic Times)*

"On an average, I spend at least 12 hours in front of the computer and by the time I get home, I feel completely beat. Lately, I have also felt a kind of lethargy settling in and I just don't feel like doing anything," a Mumbai based programmer said.

Most health experts suggest that the best remedy for burnout among techies is nipping it in the bud. Essentially, this means that techies need to strike a balance between professional and personal life, ensuring that one is not compromised for the other and the all-consuming feeling needs to make way for moderation.

Indians Want Life Beyond Work: Survey *(Times of India)*

As per an online poll conducted by market research firm AC Nielsen, 74% of Indian respondents said they preferred to be in a work that was not the all-consuming thing in their lives. A whopping 82% of those in their 20s said attaining work-life balance was a priority in the New Year.

Yes, Indian environment is different than the U.S. in some aspects and similar in some aspects. For example, the commute to work is generally longer in India, maybe not in distance but in travel time. Individual career and life aspirations, the human needs, are quite similar. Some domestic help for household chores is generally common in India but not so in the U.S. As part of my research for the Indian edition of the book, I've been having 'Balance' conversations during my yearly India trips including the 'Balance' workshops at Tata Consultency Services (TCS), Aditya Birla Group and at the Mahratta Chamber of Commerce, Industries and Agriculture.

The American edition was published 15 years ago. The Indian edition incorporates the lessons learnt over the past fifteen years as well. For the following reasons the focus of the book has shifted from 'Leadership' to 'Creativity.'

1. My research for the 'Unleashing Creativity and Innovation,' book revealed a very strong relationship between unleashing one's natural creative potential and leading a balanced life.

2. To survive and thrive in today's fast changing environment organizations need creativity at all levels and not just in the senior leadership ranks. This need creates professional growth opportunities for individuals throughout the organization.

The big personal benefit from writing the 'Balanced Life' book and facilitating workshops has been a reminder to lead a balanced life while enjoying and participating in the fast growth of my kids before they leave home for college.

Several years ago I was invited by The Indus Entrepreneurs (TiE) to speak at their annual conference in San Diego. I presented my view of critical success factors in a high-tech start-up. The gist of the presentation was that, if you want to build a lasting and successful business, then you need to provide long distance leadership. You can work sixteen hours in the short term, but eventually you will burn out. And you will be neither a creative nor effective leader in the long run. Because unresolved life-balance conflicts act as a blockage in the flow of creative intelligence. To be a long distance leader you need to understand that to lead effectively you must become a balanced person and more importantly become a good role model for your staff.

During the Q&A part after the talk one young man asked me, "Mr. Birla, looking back at your life, what are you most proud of?" My response was, "I've enjoyed a very successful and fulfilling career at FedEx, my share of stock options, cars and houses. But what I'm most thankful for is the relationship I have with my children. This is not an accident. I was present to claim my share in their joys and frustrations as they were growing up." After the Q&A, many people approached me to share a "Wish I could say that too!"

Five Lessons, Learnt So Far From My 'Balanced Life' Journey

1. We treat 'Work-Life Balance' as optional but pay a big price with what matters most – our health, relationships and professional effectiveness, especially our creative problem-solving abilities.

2. In today's fast-paced life, it is very easy to drift into an unbalanced lifestyle and not realize until it is too late that it is not the kind of life we wanted at all.

3. Is it easy? No. First, there is no such thing as enjoying a perfectly balanced life each and every day. Is it possible? Yes, a reasonable balance, for a majority of the time.

4. In today's highly competitive global economy, for companies to thrive, they must adapt and change. Creativity is the key to enterprise growth and career success in the 21st century. Looking at life from the

creativity dimension, work/career success and family life are mutually supportive.

5. As we grow, we change. We assume different roles. Our life needs change. Life is not a puzzle with only one correct fit. The puzzle pieces have to be taken apart from time to time and refitted together. Leading a balanced life is an ongoing process.

In today's fast-paced life, it is very easy to drift into an unbalanced lifestyle and not realize until it is too late that it is not the kind of life we wanted at all.

Yes, life is so very hard and so very beautiful at the same time. Let us get started on this wonderful journey for enjoying a fulfilling and balanced life in the 21st century.

❑ ❑ ❑

Chapter 2

The Tested and Proven Five-Step Process for Restoring Balance

A person has two things to aim at in life: First, to get what you want, and after that to enjoy it. Only the wisest of people achieve the second.

— Logan Pearsall Smith

While waiting in the gate area at the New Delhi airport for my flight to Mumbai, I happened to strike up a conversation with Ramesh and learned that he worked for an international advertising company in Mumbai. When he asked me the customary - "What do you do?" I told him I was an author and management consultant, and had just concluded facilitating a workshop on 'Enjoying a Balanced Life' for Microsoft managers in Bangalore.

He skeptically remarked, "I'm not sure if it is really possible to enjoy both, a successful career, as well as a fulfilling personal life. I usually work till midnight, get a few hours' sleep, get up, rush back to work, and repeat pretty much the same routine, six days a week! I haven't even seen a movie in six months!"

He continued, "I'm thirty and single, because really don't have time for a serious relationship. My diet is mostly fast food.

I don't have the luxury of thinking about the future, and I'm quite happy if I can just keep up with the commitment to my clients."

I shared, "Ramesh, I've been in your shoes and know how important your career is to you, particularly at this stage in life. Let me ask you, 'What's the single most important thing you can do for your clients?'"

Without hesitation he responded, "Come up with creative ideas."

I then asked him, "Are you familiar with the term 'brown-out'?"

"I'm not 100% sure…"

"Have you ever noticed light bulbs dimming during summer days? This happens when there's a higher demand for electricity and the power plants can't keep up with the increased load. Well, this is called a 'brown-out'. The same thing happens to us when our brains get over loaded and come under stress. In these conditions the mind no longer functions at peak capacity."

Ramesh responded with a measure of surprise in his voice, "Now that you mention it, when I started my career in advertising four years ago, I was much more creative. Now, I have lots more experience but I'm not as creative anymore!"

"Ramesh, when you get better at balancing your personal and professional lives, you are in fact positioning yourself for greater success at work. A stress free mind is naturally more creative."

An agent at the departure gate made the boarding announcement; we exchanged business cards and thanked each other for the conversation. Aboard the flight, when I looked at Ramesh's business card, I noticed that his job title was 'Creative.'

A recent top graduate in 'International Business' began his job interviews, not with discussions of opportunities for advancement, but with questions about how the companies promoted a well-balanced personal lifestyle.

A senior systems analyst at a small company has passed up numerous chances to move to larger companies at higher salaries because of the peace of mind he has as a single parent knowing his two children are nearby in the company child care center.

Statistics indicate that the very nature of the work force continues to change in ways that make balanced life concerns more critical.

In the next few years, two-thirds of new entrants into the work force will be women. Two-thirds of those women expect to become pregnant during their working years, and 40 percent expect to become responsible for aging parents.

Neither the "fast track" nor the "Mommy track" will meet these changing needs adequately.

The traditional "fast track" demands long days, short weekends and subjugation of personal and family life due to corporate interests.

The "Mommy track," described by researcher Felice Schwartz in 1989, defines a limited work role for those persons who wish to parent while continuing to work.

Neither track acknowledges certain realities:

> Workers who neglect their personal and family concerns often become less productive at work — no matter how many hours they spend there.

- Single working parents are often both "Mommy" and "Daddy."

- Many significant contributions to the workplace will be lost by relegating family-oriented workers to the restricted role of the "Mommy track."

In the media: Television and magazine ads, long recognized as windows on our culture, are reflecting balanced-life concerns. A recent magazine ad for IBM featured the headline:

"The first computer to understand you don't just have a job, you have a life."

The ad goes on to identify "trying to strike a better balance between the work you do and the life you lead" as the newest national pastime!

Faith Popcorn's best-seller, The Popcorn Report, describes trends in the culture that will influence marketing over the next decade. Terms such as "cocooning," "cashing out" and "corporate soul" reflect people's increasing needs for privacy, growing disenchantment with the culture of sushi and BMWs and rising concerns over a corporation's mission in society, as well as its profit-and-loss statement.

New businesses, unheard of only a few years ago, are providing services such as shopping, bill paying, closet organizing, and gift buying so that people can have a little time left at the end of the day.

Among teenagers: A recent survey conducted by the Bedford Kent Youth Group indicated that quality-of-life concerns — family, friends, community, time to relax, and time to do good — are more important to teenagers than fast fortunes. The same survey indicated that family relationships are rated by teenagers as very important.

Among women: Time magazine reported that 73 percent of women surveyed complained of too little leisure activity (as did 51 percent of men) and that helping women balance work and family was identified as the most important goal of the women's movement today. Concerns with helping women achieve corporate success have been replaced by concerns with helping them to achieve life success and to have the time to enjoy it!

Feminist Gloria Steinem's newest book turns to the journey within. She describes her personal search for self-worth and reveals that being admired, successful, and a nationally known leader did not guarantee a feeling of personal well-being.

She does not, however, advocate a return to the Mom-at-home and Dad-at-work solution of the Fifties. Ms. Steinem acknowledges that personal growth and relationships work together with social and political change and professional achievement to create a climate in which people of both genders can be successful and make a contribution to the world.

'Meditations For Women Who Do Too Much', by Anne Wilson Schaef, provides 365 days' worth of messages for women whose life has gotten somehow out of hand. The sheer number of women represented through the quotes and life experiences is staggering. The theme for February 5 is "exhaustion." It begins with the amusing quote from Charlotte Linton:

"Whatever women do they must do twice as well as men to be thought half as good. Luckily, this is not difficult." In trying to "do it all," women have indeed become exhausted. Exhaustion is a very real signal that one's life is out of balance.

Among men: The media also reflects changing roles and needs of men. In November 1989, Esquire magazine produced a handbook about child-rearing!

Full-page ads show fathers as well as mothers holding diapered infants. The uninvolved father in a business suit is no longer the primary role model upon which major advertising campaigns are built.

In 1990, psychologist Marvin Kinder traded his Jaguar for a second-hand Acura and wrote a book about his and his clients' experiences in choosing simpler, more balanced lifestyles. In addition to describing others who, like himself, made major and dramatic changes, he also discusses the advantages of less obvious changes such as reaching professional plateaus.

Instead of viewing a slowing of upward mobility as an indicator of professional deterioration, he encourages people to use it as an opportunity.

> Plateaus can be turned into periods of tremendous growth by using the time and energy for rest and rejuvenation, polishing neglected skills, developing new relationships, re-evaluating goals and values, and planning for long-term growth and development.

If so many of us so strongly feel the need for leading a balanced life — then why aren't more of us achieving it? We have become slaves to our work, our expectations, our possessions, our mortgage payments. We are intelligent, capable, and sensitive people. Why can we not seem to gain control over our own lives?

> We want to have a balanced and healthy lifestyle, but we do not know how because we are not born with the secret of how to live.

1. We do not know how

The modern lifestyle requires skills that our parents and even some of our mentors did not have or need to have. To develop balanced-life skills requires that we be willing to be patient, to experiment, and to make a commitment to continuously update our skills and information.

2. We procrastinate

We mean to get back to these balanced-life concerns but we have bills to pay, things to do, career opportunities to seize, planes to catch, and activities to pursue. Before we know it another year has passed. We avoid dealing with balanced-life issues directly, but they never quite seem to go away.

3. We employ unhealthy substances and strategies to manage the stress caused by an unbalanced lifestyle.

• Chemicals: I need a drink!

In the United States, the top two prescription drugs are not antibiotics or birth-control pills. They are two different types of tranquilizers. Although tranquilizers and other prescription drugs have many appropriate, helpful and healthful uses, they may become simply another means of avoiding the balanced-life issues that created the stress in the first place.

Consider Bill's story: Bill was a 30-year-old minister with a wife in graduate school, a new baby and the relentlessly busy Christmas season approaching. He had been unable to shake a chronic cough and cold, and went to his physician for medication to get him back on his feet so he could resume his duties. Before the physical exam, the physician took a detailed life history, including current health habits, responsibilities and stresses. Instead of the expected prescription for strong antibiotics, Bill received advice on a change in diet, an exercise plan and strategies for stress management. Accompanied by a mild cough medicine, this "prescription" made a difference, not only in Bill's cough but also in his life!

- **Living in the future: Everything will be fine just as soon as I... get the promotion, build the house, etc.**

The problem with this coping strategy is that the future, by definition, never arrives. The new job, house, boat or spouse rarely bring the longed-for satisfaction, and the race goes on. It is good to have goals, but always looking to the future stops us from living in the present. One important lesson often learned by those facing serious illness is that every day is valuable for itself and not just as a means to tomorrow's achievements. Life has to be lived today.

- **Projection: I'm doing it for them.**

We know our life is out of balance, but we rationalize that we are providing more material things for our families. If we took time to ask our children and spouse what they really want, we might be surprised at the answers. Consider the responses of a group of business executives when asked to give a two-minute talk about themselves. The exercise was an "ice breaker" speech at the meeting of a civic club. The executives talked about happy memories of childhood, fishing trips with dad, family camping trips, summer at the beach, school plays, and piano recitals.

> Every day is valuable for itself and not just as a means to tomorrow's achievements. Life has to be lived today.

No one talked about the kind of clothes they wore, the kind of house they lived in, the expensive toys they played with or the make and model of the family car. When asked to tell about who they were, the executives talked about shared experiences and happy memories of themselves.

- **Externalizing: I need a new job.**

Changing jobs, locations, cars or houses may be helpful if it is the sincere desire for the new job, location, car or house that motivates the change. Change, however, may also be used to avoid problems that need to be resolved.

Consider Mark's story: Mark was telling a friend over lunch about his recent physical. The doctor had suggested that Mark change jobs to reduce stress and the resulting high-blood pressure.

The friend remarked, "Maybe it will help, and maybe it will not.

Even in the new job, you are going to take Mark wherever you go."

Ultimately, Mark decided to change the job. At last report, however, his family did not like the move, and he is thinking of moving again.

- **Compensating : What I really need is a new... house, car, boat, etc.**

We feel that something is missing but instead of finding out which one of our balanced-life needs is going unmet, we listen to the media and try to fill the empty space with increased material consumption: designer clothes, gourmet food, sophisticated sound equipment, faster cars, etc. Such things give temporary relief from the symptoms, but the real problem keeps eating at the stomach lining.

- **Fatalism: I guess that's the price for success.**

The day after Jack got the big promotion he had sought so frantically for three years, his wife decided to file for divorce. Jack was disappointed, but shrugged it off, saying, "I guess that's the price of success." Instead of looking within and coming to terms with his unbalanced life, he simply resigned himself to the easy excuse of a false reality.

- **Disengagement: There's nothing I can do.**

Disengagement is a frequent consequence of workers finding themselves in a professional plateau or other situation in which promotion, salary increase or job growth seems impossible. To compensate for the lack of anticipated rewards and to balance the scale, the amount of effort expended is simply reduced. The worker resigns without actually quitting the job. She or he simply reduces effort, involvement and creativity. Dana resigned from her job without leaving the office! A regular cycle of three-year promotions came to an end after she had risen to a position in which her immediate superior was a young person unlikely to leave or retire within the near future. So Dana simply maintained the status quo and resisted any new or creative ideas that demanded more effort. The result was that her need to be challenged at work was unmet, and she began to experience a feeling of diminished success off the job as well.

- **Avoidance: I just need to finish one more project and then I'll relax.**

The above quote could easily be made by a confirmed workaholic the day before the massive heart attack signals that he or she has finished too many projects already. The different parts of the total self send signals through the body, mind and spirit when life gets out of balance: the nagging headaches, backaches, restlessness; the feeling that something's missing but you can't put your finger on it.

These experiences are trying to tell us, "Hey! Something's out of balance!"— much as the buzzer on an automatic washing machine signals loudly that the load has become unbalanced and needs attention. If we responded as quickly to the signals of our body and mind as we do to the buzzing of the washing machine, balanced-life issues would be resolved much more easily.

Other people also send us signals, if only we will listen. How many times in the past week have you put off your child, spouse, parent or friend with the excuse of "Just as soon as I finish this."?

• **Passivity: It's out of my control.**

Another common coping mechanism is to play the passive or victim role and blame a lack of balanced life on a supervisor who expects too much, the length of the "to do" list at home, non-supportive spouse, demanding children, etc.

Phrases such as "What can I do?" or "It's out of my control," or "I've tried everything," indicate passivity. This rationalization may bring temporary relief from trying to solve the problem, but the pressure continues to build.

• **Analyzing, intellectualizing: I/you should be happy.**

Statements regarding how another person "should" feel are often made by someone who hasn't a clue as to how she or he (or anyone else) is actually feeling!

A focus on logical and concrete events ignores the emotional, personal, and spiritual components of life. The media and society reinforce this approach by implying, "If you have everything, you should be happy."

Dick, a very successful business executive, became distraught upon finding out that his wife had become an alcoholic. "I just don't understand," he said. "I make good money. We live in a beautiful house, drive imported cars, and have a nice portfolio."

In Dick's mind, with all these things, there was no excuse for Marsha to be depressed and resort to alcohol. He had ignored the importance of his wife's definition of success, which included emotional, relational and spiritual well-being, as well as material affluence.

What is the Healthy Way to Deal with Balanced-Life Issues?

The power to lead a balanced lifestyle is within each one of us. Before we can tap that power, we have to give up the victim role and take responsibility for our lives. We have to reclaim our lives from the habits, expectations, roles, people and situations that keep us frustrated and unfulfilled. When we truly understand and accept this responsibility, then we are on our way to a successful life journey.

> Where we are today in our lives is a summation of all the countless choices — big and small — that we have made. Where we will be in 10 years begins with the choices we make today.

You have brains in your head. You have feet in your shoes. You can steer yourself any direction you choose.

- Dr. Seuss

Each one of us is unique in aspirations, achievements, frustrations and environments. There cannot be one solution that will apply to all situations. If someone gives you a "canned" or ready-made formula for balanced life, be very cautious.

The process presented here for addressing and managing balanced-life issues is one that should help you develop solutions that fit the uniqueness of your environment. As you grow and your life changes, new approaches will be required to help keep your life in balance.

A proven process for making 'work-life balance' promoting choices

Celebrating life in its fullness, one week at a time
Visualize whole. Start small. Act now

1. **V**isualize a balanced week and choose one activity you're not doing now
2. **I**dentify internal and external roadblocks
3. **D**evelop action steps to overcome the roadblocks
4. **E**ngage stakeholders in your implementation support system
5. **O**utline the reason why you want to (must) make this change

As you'll notice the acronym for this five-step process is V.I.D.E.O. Following the 5-Step Process lets us enjoy Work-Life Balance today but also build virtual videos stored in the human hard drive/mind's DVR - memories for tomorrow. Isn't this the best gift we can give to our loved ones?

"You build wonderful memories and you build a life that way."

Happy Montgomery, of Spartanburg, and sister Irene Tzouvelekas, of Greenville, took their annual trip to Litchfield Beach to rent a house with their children and grandchildren. But instead of bringing five cars including a big van, this year they brought three, including a hybrid Honda Fit, which, "to fill the gas tank slap full only costs $35", Montgomery explained. The clan also cut down on eating out.

This year she plans to skip her usual trip to Europe but vows never to do away with the summer getaway.

"You build memories," she said, relaxing on a bench with her sister at a Myrtle Beach mall. "You build wonderful memories and you build a life that way."

Earthlink Main News, July 23, 2008

We treat life balance as optional but pay a high price in what matters most – relationships, health, career ...

Unmet life-balance needs create conflicts within and with the people we love. Conflicts generate stress.

"What I fear most about stress is not that it kills, but that it prevents one from savoring life."

The Art of Time, Jean - Louis Servan-Schreiber

When the system is not at ease = Dis-ease

Boss' #1:Business' need is creative ideas, the key to career success in the 21st century

A stressed mind is not in a creative mode. A stressed mind is in a survival mode.

During my March 2016 India visit I facilitated a three-hour work-life balance conversation for a group of 20 professionals, organized by the Mahratta Chamber of Commerce in Pune. I split the large group into four small groups numbered one to four and gave them the following four questions.

Group 1: What is the impact of an unbalanced lifestyle on your personal life?

Group 2: What is the impact of an unbalanced lifestyle on your professional life?

Group 3: What gets in the way of enjoying a balanced life?

Group 4: What strategies or steps you've used successfully to restore balance?

Group 1 shared the following as to the impact of an unbalanced lifestyle on personal life.

- No time for people we love
- Stress leading to health issues
- Constant feeling of frustration
- Going into depression
- Lack of satisfaction in life
- Lack of motivation at work

Do we have the resources to lead a balanced life?

Absolutely yes!

Why should we bother now?

There is no dress rehearsal in this life. We do not get a second chance. We have to live and enjoy the life as we go along.

Don't underestimate the power of small changes in producing big results.

A tiny delicate flower may seem insignificant by itself but can color a hillside in sufficient numbers.

> A fulfilling life is not just one or two big achievements. Simple day-to-day joys and shared experiences can add up to a well-lived and meaningful life.

The next five chapters will focus on application of the five-step V.I.D.E.O. process.

❑ ❑ ❑

Chapter 3

Visualize the Balanced Healthy State: The First Step

Dost thou love life? Then do not squander time, for that is the stuff life is made of.

- Benjamin Franklin

Defining Balance in the 21st Century

In the 20th century, the 'Work-Life Balance' conversation centered about balancing the hours spent on the job with the hours dedicated to personal/family life – i.e. work from 8 to 5, and once home, detach from work and enjoy your personal/family activities. Today with 24x7connectivity, we no longer see a clear separation between 'work time' and 'personal time'. Smartphones, laptops and other mobile devices make it very easy to receive and respond to work emails at any hour, from any place. That usually means checking on emails after the kids have gone to bed.

To better reflect today's inescapable reality of trying to fit together various life roles and responsibilities for success on and off the job, the American Psychological Association and the Society for Human Resource Management have started to use the term **'work-life fit.'**

"Yet, when it comes to balancing work with family and personal life, he doesn't think our obsession with our devices is helping. He doesn't believe in work/life "balance" but in **work/life harmony**. There is no such thing as balance. It's how do I harmonize my work and my life?"

**Satya Nadella, Microsoft CEO,
The Times of India, April 10, 2016**

While attending graduate school in Chicago I was invited by a church to speak on vegetarianism. To help prepare for the talk, my roommate Chandra Kant Shah gave me a book by the Jain muni (ascetic) Chitrabhanu. I liked Gurudeo Chitrabhanu's message and made it a point to visit his New York center during my business trips to the city. He was gracious to bless us with visits and talks in Indianapolis and Memphis. During one of our evening walks in Memphis, I asked him, "Gurudeo, what's the purpose of life?" With some reflection he said, "Purpose of life is to celebrate life in its fullness." The derivation - 'Goal of balanced life is to celebrate life in its fullness' - became my guiding and operating mantra.

> "Gurudeo, what's the purpose of life?" With some reflection he said, "Purpose of life is to celebrate life in its fullness." The derivation - 'Goal of balanced life is to celebrate life in its fullness' - became my guiding and operating mantra.

The obvious follow-up question to Gurudeo's response is, "What constitutes fullness?" This chapter explores in detail the answer to this very important question. The constituents of fullness can be viewed from many perspectives. One perspective is 'life roles', i.e. balancing the limited time available to us to celebrate and enjoy all our life roles. The balancing process becomes increasingly demanding as more and more life roles are assumed – professional (career), spouse, parent (family), friend, mentor, tennis player, gym partner, etc.... We will discover that when viewed in isolation, on and off-the-job roles may appear in conflict but when viewed holistically as being integrated, they are in fact, complementary.

When we choose well-being for the whole, the pay-off is always greater. Multiple roles turn into multiple sources of joy. Leading a balanced life is intentionally making choices that support wholeness, and therefore, celebrate life in its fullness.

I'm a musician, but I'm also a father, a husband, a son, a citizen, an African American, an American – and at the root of all that, I'm a human being. My vision comes from my humanity, not from my being a musician. That opens it up, completely removes any walls.

- Herbie Hancock
Musician; Winner of multiple Academy
and Grammy Awards

WHAT ARE WE AFTER IN LIFE? This is the first question asked of business and professional leaders in the Leadership and Balanced Life seminar conducted by the author. Responses of participants usually reflect themes of happiness, success, sense-of-contribution, love, making money, financial security, and self-fulfillment.

Discussion on the follow-up question ("Why do you want happiness, success, money...") frequently generates the response: "Because it makes me feel good about myself." This discussion is followed by the request that participants write down the things, activities, and accomplishments that have made them feel good about themselves within the past year.

> Before reading further, complete the exercise yourself: Write down the experiences, activities and accomplishments that have made you feel good within the past year. (Don't cheat and skip ahead to the next section. This is important!)

Now, compare your responses to those of other business and professional leaders who have completed this exercise. (The notations following each response will be explained later in the chapter.) As you'll see from the similarity in responses of participants, both, in India and the U.S that we all feel happy when common needs are met, i.e. universal human needs.

Responses of workshop participants in India

These are from 'Work-Life Balance' seminar/conversations at Microsoft, Bangalore; Tata Consulting Services (TCS,) Noida and Gurgaon; Aditya Birla Group, Mumbai, and Mahratta Chamber of Commerce, Pune.

Anuja

1. Travelling on holiday – to areas with beautiful nature (A/L)
2. Enjoying a beautiful film with my family (P)
3. Enjoying moments of success in small things (C)
4. Sitting in a garden and enjoying a nice book (L)
5. Enjoying food made by mother, husband and my kids (P)
6. Being at home and relaxing (L)
7. Memorizing good moments in life (C/P/A/L)

Kunal

1. CFA charter completion (C/A)

2. Being able to work in difficult types of projects (C)
3. Appreciation for my work (C)
4. Scuba Diving (L)
5. Social work for mid-day meals etc. (A)
6. Wife becoming an accomplished teacher (P)
7. Opportunity to travel (within/outside India) (L)

Mandhar

1. Professionally last one year was good (c)
2. I took a two-week break and trekked in Manali-Hampta pass. There was no mobile or email and I was in nature's company with my son and wife and other group members (P/L)
3. Playing with my daughter after work has been enjoyable (P)
4. My mother expired last year and it gives me satisfaction that I was by her side always and being an entrepreneur I could always manage my schedule and be by her side when she needed me (A)
5. Weekend outdoor trips with kids and family gave me immense joy (P/A/L)

Kalyani

1. Climbing highest peak in Maharashtra was a great accomplishment for me (A/L)
2. Got job at Aditya Birla Group (C)
3. Called by my MBA college to share my international experience with juniors (L)
4. Met my life partner in college (P)
5. Completed my MBA (A/C)

Shraddha

1. When I cracked my biggest deal (C)
2. When I cook for family (P/L)
3. Conversations with friends (P)
4. When I planted my garden (L)
5. Playing with my nephew (P)
6. When we've (me and husband) relaxing, long conversations over a drink (P)

Pooja

1. ABGLP Summit Success (C)
2. Regular workout and diet (L)
3. Paris Trip (L)
4. Going out with friends (P)
5. Toastmasters – delivering a speech (A)
6. Taking my parents out (P)

Shukla

1. Travel to Goa beach and relaxing (L)
2. Meditation and prayer (A)
3. Daily puja, recitation of shlokas (A)
4. Going to office and returning home (C)
5. Meeting close friends and relatives (P)
6. Good fresh vegetarian food (L)

Tejas

1. Celebrating birthday surprise planned by spouse (P)
2. Going on a vacation/exploring new places (L)

3. Getting appreciated for good work by bosses (C)

4. Being part of designing/creating something new at work (C)

5. Getting promoted at work (C)

6. Playing my favorite sport after a really long time (L)

Anandita

1. A holiday with my family (P)

2. Publishing my own short story and book in the international market (A)

3. Completing the new HR manual in my company (C)

4. Cooking different cuisines (L/A)

5. Joining a singing and dance class (L/A)

Responses of workshop participants in the United States

Cecilia —Psychologist in private practice:

1. Working with increasing number of child/family clients in my practice (C/A)

2. Sewing French dresses for my daughters (P)

3. Reading some good books (L)

4. Discussing with my husband new ideas he gained during his study (P/A)

5. Getting reconnected with old and new friends at Rhodes Forum (P)

6. Church activities (A)

Madan — Federal Express Executive:

1. Playing tennis twice a week (L)

2. Evening walks with wife (P)

3. Attending my daughter's softball games (P)
4. Son graduating from school in top 10 percent of his class (P)
5. Sunday (religious) school activities (A)
6. Assuming more responsibility at work (C)

David — Sonoco Products:

1. Introduced a new quality-improvement program at work (C)
2. Successfully reduced our plant's budget by $25,000 (C)
3. Visited South Carolina, Louisiana, Florida for pleasure (L)
4. Had the best Christmas with my family in years (P)
5. Saw my sister after a two-year absence (P)
6. More involved with the local food bank and organ transplant center (A)

Susan — Fogelman Executive Center at University of Memphis:

1. Recognition from employer for hard work done on a major project (C)
2. Love and support from family and friends (P)
3. Inner strength, which carried me through some rough spots (A)
4. Faith in God (A)
5. Renovation of my new (older) home (L)

Ron — Dow Corning Wright:

1. Solving a difficult situation at work (C)

2. Relating well with my daughters and wife (P)

3. Helping my children with homework (P)

4. Having a good relationship with church friends (P)

5. Having extra income to use for travel (L)

6. Hearing a good sermon (A)

Debbie — Peabody Hotel:

1. Trip to Nashville with husband and kids (P/L)

2. Exceeded my own sales goals at work (C)

3. Planned several events at work that went very well — happy clients (C)

4. Started aerobics classes in June and kept with it (L)

5. Lost weight, so look a little better (L/A)

6. Managed to live through another X-mas season both professionally and personally without a nervous breakdown (A)

Bill — South Central Bell:

1. Good friends — friendship with some have gotten stronger, I help them and they help me (P)

2. Successful completion of several major projects at work (C)

3. Received good evaluation, pay raise and bonus (C)

4. Relationship with my girlfriend (P)

5. Playing in several concerts. I enjoy playing the saxophone (L)

6. Growing relationship with God (A)

Why did people write these things down? Why did you answer as you did?

People feel good when a need is satisfied. When we are thirsty, drinking cold water feels good — satisfaction of a physical need. The same is true of psychological needs.

The preceding responses show that the psychological self is multi-dimensional, that a multitude of things/experiences are important to satisfying our psychological needs. It is not a coincidence that each list contains items that address one or more of the following needs: (C) career; (P) people; (A) actualization;(L) leisure.

This is true despite the fact that respondents were quite dissimilar in age, occupation, income and professional/business specialty. People feel fulfilled when important human needs are satisfied.

NEEDS	SOURCES OF SATISFACTION (need satisfiers)	SPECIFIC REWARDS
Recognition/esteem: "I want to be somebody."	CAREER	Power, social status, recognition, leadership opportunities, money.
Love, belonging: "I want to be somebody to somebody"	PEOPLE	Mutual support, attention, affection, sexuality and sensuality, group membership, shared experiences, communication.

Identity, self-respect "I want to be somebody to myself."	ACTUALIZATION	Being in touch with the physical, emotional, mental and spiritual environment; reaching goals we set for ourselves; sense of meaning and coherence in life.
Physical, relaxation: "I want a break from the pressures of being/ becoming somebody."	LEISURE	Activities chosen just for fun" and not for making a living; recharging one's batteries.

What this exercise tells us is that we need to examine our life experiences to see for ourselves what leads to fulfillment/ happiness and what leads to conflict/stress. We don't have to accept blindly the wisdom of how-to books or psychologists. We have the raw material: life experiences. What we need is time for reflection and introspection.

Interestingly enough, the real-life observations reflected in the author's surveys are consistent with the findings of well-known psychologists, such as Abraham Maslow, Carl Rogers and William Glasser. These researchers have devoted much of their study to the functioning of healthy individuals, identifying ways to help "normal" individuals function more effectively.

We need to examine our life experiences to see for ourselves what leads to fulfillment/happiness and what leads to conflict/stress. We don't have to accept blindly the wisdom of how-to books or psychologists.

Physical/Relaxation Needs

Abraham Maslow studied healthy people in the belief that healthy people can teach others about higher levels of human awareness and ways to achieve them. He described five primary sets of needs that motivate human behavior: physiological, safety/security, love and belongingness, esteem, and self-actualization. These needs are arranged in a hierarchical fashion, because the basic survival needs must be satisfied before others can be addressed.

The basic physiological needs are food, water, air, and shelter. Although leisure, physical exercise and relaxation were not includedin Maslow's original list, physical well-being is clearly indicated as an important human need.

Physical and relaxation needs are often relegated to the "back burner" in modern society until the body clearly signals its distress through a heart attack or ulcer. Suddenly, at that point, making time for exercise becomes a life-giving necessity rather than a low-priority frill.

Taking care of our bodies through nutrition, exercise, rest and relaxation enables us to address our needs for recognition, belonging and identity more effectively.

Love/Belonging Needs

According to William Glasser, the difference between psychologically healthy people and others is based on whether or not an individual has a "success identity" or a "failure identity." This identity is developed through interaction with others as others provide feedback.

An integral part of this interpersonal transaction is the need to love and be loved — "I am somebody to somebody." People who are successful at motivating others — managers, teachers, coaches, parents — have been applying these principles successfully for years.

Glasser's concept of "success identity" is important to the development of recognition and esteem needs as well.

Recognition/Esteem Needs

Esteem needs consist of the desires for reputation and respect from others. Psychologist Carl Rogers uses the term "unconditional positive regard" to describe the experience of being valued for what one is, rather than for what one should be or ought to be; being valued for being as well as for doing; being recognized for one's strengths rather than for one's weaknesses.

Human beings of all ages need such experiences if they are to realize their potentials and develop their talents and abilities. Successful leaders and managers know this and use this skill in helping their employees identify and utilize their strengths, rather than berating them for their failures.

Esteem and respect from others provide a foundation for self-esteem and self-respect, and point the way toward attainment of the highest level of human awareness: self-actualization.

Self-Actualization

Carl Rogers also writes of the drive to achieve psychological maturity, which he believed to be deeply rooted in human nature. Important questions in personal growth are "How can I become what I deeply wish to become?" and "How can I get behind my facades and become myself?"

These questions are also contained in Maslow's concept of self-actualization, which includes a person's desire to reach his or her potential in a multi dimensional way: personal, social, occupational, physical, and spiritual.

The experience of self-actualization is more than just achieving a singular personal, corporate or financial goal. It is the experience of feeling that one is exercising a unique and precious combination of skills and abilities; that one is fulfilling a special purpose of making a special contribution; and that one's life is connected to a larger sense of purpose or meaning.

> Self-actualization is more than just achieving a singular personal, corporate or financial goal. It is the experience of feeling that one is exercising a unique and precious combination of skills and abilities; that one is fulfilling a special purpose of making a special contribution; and that one's life is connected to a larger sense of purpose or meaning.

Spiritual development, a central part of self-actualization, is defined by people in many ways. Although the term "spiritual" is often used by people with formal religious affiliation, it is a universal human experience.

Jean Grasso Fitzpatrick defines the word spiritual as "an awareness of our sacred connection with all of life," and spiritual nurture as "the opportunity to share with our children something more enduring than the hope of success or even happiness." If we are to have this "something" to share with children or others whom we care about, we must take the time to develop or nurture it within ourselves.

Most 2-year-olds know intuitively how to focus attention. When speaking to a distracted adult, they will often take your face between their hands and turn it toward theirs, thereby gaining your undivided attention. Five minutes of such undivided attention is worth more than hours of half-hearted inattention, whether we are giving it to ourselves or to others.

Anne Wilson Schaef acknowledged this important reality in writing her book, Meditations for Women Who Do Too Much. Each day's meditation is less than a page in length, and most take less than a minute to read. Using such are source daily, only five minutes per day, a person could add 30 hours of spiritual nurture to each year of his or her life.

Theologian Frederick Buechner puts the matter succinctly: Pay attention to your life.

If we are to pay attention to our lives, we must not be paying attention to half a dozen other things as well. Clearing out the mind for even a few moments each day is a good beginning for the lifelong process of spiritual development and self-actualization.

The Balanced Life Model

The Balanced Life Model incorporates the fundamental psychological concepts of human needs as motivators, the presence of an innate drive toward psychological maturity, and the importance of identity for psychological health and personal success.

This model represents the integration of the author's work in management and leadership training with the basic psychological principles described above. It is a multi-dimensional model that can be illustrated graphically:

The Balanced Life Model has eight key characteristics. The following case studies show how the model operates in real-life situations.

1. The total self must be regarded not as a collection of isolated components, but as one integrated whole

Consider Bill's story. He joined his division two years before as a manager of planning, is good at what he does and had always been a positive leader. Recently, however, he had become openly critical of management and very negative in general. A colleague noticed the change and approached Bill about it.

COLLEAGUE: Bill, is there something I can help you with? You have not been your positive self lately.

BILL: You're right. When I joined the department two years ago, I was promised that I would be reporting to the Vice President — my boss's boss. Now, when I ask for that, I am told that no such promise was made.

COLLEAGUE: It is obvious that this is bothering you very much. If the reporting level is that important to you, then maybe you need to change jobs. This may mean moving, since other industries in your field are out of state.

BILL: I don't want to move. I like the neighborhood we live in and the church we attend. We all like living only an hour away from both my parents and my wife's parents. I enjoy coaching the boys' soccer team and playing golf without having to spend a fortune doing it. I also like the people in my department and the peers I work with.

COLLEAGUE: The only thing you really don't like about your life is the reporting level in the organization, and to change that you may have to sacrifice other things you like.

BILL: That's a different way to look at the situation.

COLLEAGUE (some time later): The holistic look at the situation made Bill think, and I noticed a change in him, back to being a positive leader.

DISCUSSION: When making career decisions, the tendency is to look at career in isolation from other aspects of life. Decisions and choices made in this way are not the optimum choices in terms of overall life fulfillment. As Bill's situation illustrates, such a narrow decision-making focus may also be destructive to a career as well!

REFLECTION: Take a moment to look at your whole life — the big picture. In each of the four areas (Career, People, Actualizing, and Leisure) write down what is satisfying to you.

2. Expansion in one component cannot compensate for a missing component

Last week Mark finally got the position he had been working for: Vice President of Sales. The same week, his wife asked him for a divorce. Mark was devastated and said to his friends, "I just want one more chance to prove that I can be a good husband and father. I'll change jobs. I'll change towns."

DISCUSSION: Mark had let himself become "married to the job" and did not have any time for his wife. His situation illustrates the fact that career advancements are satisfying and fulfilling to the Career Self but cannot compensate for fulfillment of the People Self. It took a tragic event to bring this to Mark's attention!

REFLECTION: Look at your calendar. How much time is devoted to the important people/relationships in your life?

3. Only the individual can define for himself or herself the scope and sources of fulfillment within each of the four components of the balanced life circle

A month after attending the Leadership and Balanced Life seminar, Jane phoned the leader to say she had some good news to announce: "I just called to let you know that I declined a promotion!"

By using the Balanced Life Model to evaluate the total life impact of accepting versus not accepting the promotion, Jane came to the conclusion that at this point in time she was happier without the added pressure. The job involved 50 percent travel. With two pre-teen daughters, Jane did not wish to be away from home that much. Although everyone in her department was pressuring her to take the job, she felt happy and satisfied in declining it at this time.

DISCUSSION: Jane did not fall into the trap of allowing other people to define her life needs and sources of satisfaction. Although accepting the promotion might have been a very fruitful decision for another of her colleagues, it was not best for Jane at the time. She used the expanded definition of "success" and the Balanced Life Model to evaluate the impact of a decision in one area of life upon her life as a whole. Not only will she be a happier person, but she will also perform better at work when her whole life is in balance.

REFLECTION: What is an important decision facing you right now? How will that decision impact your life as a whole (Career, People, Actualizing, Leisure)?

4. Each Component Has Its Own Joys and Disappointments

Ann was devastated when the doctor told her that "tennis elbow" was acting up and that she should give up playing for a while. She reacted as though she'd been told she had only a few months to live. Her children remarked that she looked as if she'd just lost her best friend.

Ann has been frustrated for several years at her under-stimulating job and has also felt less needed at home as her two children entered their pre-teen years. So tennis had become her avenue for accomplishment and achievement.

She devoted herself diligently to the game and became quite good at it. She became so good, in fact, that she neglected other areas of her life. She literally lived all week for her weekend matches, and her mood for the week was usually determined by her "score" of the previous weekend. In her own eyes, Ann's tennis score reflected the sum total of her self-worth.

Yes, most of the imbalance in life is a result of the work demands. But excessive dedication to other part of the whole-self can also result in an unbalanced life. Volunteering is good and a positive expression of the spiritual/actualizing self. But excessive volunteering can eat into family time. Participating in children's sports activities is good and meets children's extremely important 'I matter' psychological needs/people self. But parents trying to live their life through children's accomplishments on the field can put too much pressure on themselves and the children.

Twenty-eight-year-old Dan was devastated when the mental-health center to which he had devoted the past five years of his life suddenly lost its funding and began laying off employees. His work had been his source of career development, leisure time activity, personal friendship and self-esteem. He socialized, worked and played with co-workers, and had few interests outside his work and colleagues.

The layoffs threatened not only his own job security but also the close knit social system to which he belonged. More than his career was at stake here. Dan saw his whole life hanging in the balance of administrative decisions made by others.

DISCUSSION: The Career Self provides joy through challenges and sense of accomplishment but it also provides disappointments. Leisure activities provide relaxation and challenges but also frustrations. The point is that no one part of the self can provide all of life's kicks all of the time. Once we understand that, then we don't put all our eggs in one basket by investing all our time and energy in just one part of the self.

REFLECTION: Close your eyes and imagine for a moment what your life would be like if you had only your career to meet your needs. What would your life be like without leisure, people, or actualization experiences?

5. Each Component is Supportive of the Others in Both Success and Failure

Asha got the big promotion! She immediately called her husband and best friend and announced the date for the celebration. The satisfaction of his business success was

The recent proliferation of corporate gyms and health programs is not just a reflection of increased health-consciousness. It is also a reflection of the increased productivity that is seen in healthy employees. Good health and good relationships make economic sense as well as personal sense.

multiplied when it was shared with others. How much less satisfying it might have been if there had been no one to call with the good news?

DISCUSSION: It is a well-documented fact that individuals with supportive and understanding relationships are better able to withstand the stresses of the modern-day, fast-paced lifestyle. The Balanced Life Model is made up of two halves: Career (C) and Personal(PAL). The Personal life is not in conflict with the Career (C) but in fact is very supportive (hence, the letters PAL!) The personal relationships, self-actualization and leisure activities are not in competition with career development, but work together as a supportive unit.

REFLECTION: Have you ever had some good news, phoned a friend and found the line busy? Remember your disappointment and frustration? This experience illustrates the important support role of each part of the Balanced Life Model. Success is sweeter and failure more bearable if there are friends and family members with whom to share it.

6. The ceiling to one's personal happiness is set by the component of lowest satisfaction

George was eating a delicious Mexican dinner with two colleagues in a beautiful restaurant in downtown San Antonio. He had just made a successful presentation at a prestigious professional conference.

George said, "Guys, I'm in the company of good friends... having just presented

a good paper... enjoying a nice meal. Why don't I feel so good?" Further discussion revealed that he was not very happy in his job, and that was stopping him from enjoying the present moment 100 percent.

DISCUSSION: A person may appear very happy in her or his work and leisure activities. If he or she is miserable in the People part of life, however, then the personal rating of overall happiness will not be much above that of the People situation. The same is true of dissatisfaction with Career or Leisure. Like George, a person may be fulfilling Actualization, People and Leisure needs, and still feel unfulfilled because the Career Self is out of balance.

REFLECTION: Stop right now and "live in the moment!" What are the satisfactions you are receiving from your career... from your people relationships... from your self-actualization... your leisure activities?

7. The components have to be taken apart from time to time and refitted together

"I can't understand it," muses Catherine, an attorney with a large corporate firm. "My friends can't understand it. Two years ago, I was the original 'party animal.' I could stay up later and go out more nights than anyone I knew, and still turn in a dynamite performance at work. I still enjoy my friends and my work, but all I want to do in the evenings now is curl up with a good book by the fire or have an occasional casual evening with a few close friends. Is something wrong?"

DISCUSSION: The distribution of energy and time to each of the four components of a balanced life has to be changed as we grow older, as life circumstances change and as the world changes. Psychologist Erik Erickson identified specific stages of adult development that are similar to the developmental stages that children experience. Gail Sheehy popularized this notion in her best seller, Passages. Faith Popcorn's recent best-seller, The Popcorn Report, identifies social trends, such as "cocooning" and describes their impact on the way people live and the products they buy.

As we grow, our needs change. Self-actualization and spiritual development take greater importance as we grow older than when we were starting our careers. The intensity of relationship needs that are prominent in young adulthood later give way to needs for productivity and then for contribution and mentoring. The task for the individual in each transition is to achieve the new balance. It is an ongoing process.

The whole idea behind developmental changes is that things can never be settled once and for all. Life is a thriller all right, but not one we can solve with one "right" set of clues. Life is not a puzzle with only one correct fit. Getting it right at 30 will not be the same as getting it right at 20. The activities that relieved stress in 2007 may accelerate stress in 2017.

REFLECTION: Compare what gives meaning to your life now with what did so 10 years ago. They are different. Why? Not because you didn't have it "right" 10 years ago, but because you and your world have changed and grown.

8. Each component has elements of others, but cannot totally substitute for the others, as each component provides its own unique fulfillment

Bill is a successful businessman, whose daily routine is coming home late, eating dinner and retiring to the study with his laptop computer and brief case.

In a recent conversation he said, "I love my job. I get a lot of satisfaction and enjoyment. I had my physical last week and the doctor was insisting that I take up a leisure activity. I don't have time for a leisure activity. My wife is also insisting on some activity we can do together."

DISCUSSION: Society in general and corporate life in particular encourages people to define their worth solely in terms of career and material success.

Since there is only so much room at the top of the corporate pyramid, this narrow definition leaves us extremely vulnerable, often feeling failed and frustrated. Extra hours spent doing work cannot substitute for the relaxation provided by leisure. Although we develop collegial relationships at work, they are not substitutes for the kind of joy provided by the more intimate family and friendship relationships.

Conclusion

This chapter began with the question: What is a balanced life, and why is it important? A balanced life is a model for living that is based on positive assumptions about human growth and motivation. A balanced life can be visualized as a balanced healthy state in which the individual uses all of his or her skills, takes charge of his or her life and celebrates life in its fullness.

In our own way, each one of us is pursuing happiness. No doubt, career success is one source of happiness. The ambition providing the drive for success is good, but a blindly ambitious person is self-destructive. A person who is never satisfied with his or her success and always keeps pushing is headed for trouble — if not in trouble already!

Here are some important questions to ask yourself:
• Whose happiness are you pursuing? Is it your own definition of success, worth and identity — or someone else's?
• Are you in touch with your own definition of "success identity" — or do you allow your boss, friends, family or the media to define your life for you?

• Does your calendar reflect the life you own, or does it appear to be someone else's?

Periodically, we need to evaluate our beliefs and goals

in light of our own life experiences and replace them with more enlightened beliefs. By paying attention to our own life experiences, we are validating whether or not our internal measure of success is truly our own or what someone else has "sold" to us.

Life experiences tell us there is no happiness without peace of mind. Being at peace with one's self means being in touch with all dimensions of the self: the changing needs; what makes you fulfilled; the directions you're taking; and, most important, the balance between the Career, People, Actualizing and Leisure aspects of your life.

> Happiness is not a result of what happens to us but what happens in us when that harmonious self within is at peace. It is folly to think that peace will come along like a cloud from the heavens. Thoughtful people generate their peace from within.

Once we get in touch with our lives as a whole and expand the definition of success, we begin to lead life differently — a life reflecting more balanced allocation of money, time and energy to the four needs of the Balanced Life Model.

It is liberating to realize that the smaller house is more fulfilling than the bigger house if the relationships inside the house are becoming deeper. It is liberating to realize that greater life fulfillment is a lifestyle that allows time to engage in leisure and self-actualization activities. It is liberating to realize that doing what you enjoy and experiencing a sense of accomplishment can be as fulfilling as a bigger title.

It is the four components — Career, People, Leisure, and Actualization— when combined, that make us whole.

Practical Application Example

Enjoying Life Today and Building Memories (V.I.D.E.O.) for Tomorrow

Personal Action Plan

Celebrating Life in its Fullness, One Week at a Time

NAME : *Madan Birla (Dual Career Couple, Daughter 8, Son 13)*

WEEK OF: *March 2*

Attend both Children's Talent Shows and after School Games and Activities

VISUALIZE: A Balanced Week and Choose One Activity You're Not Doing Now

Attend both Children's Talent Shows and after School Games and Recitals

IDENTIFY : Internal and External Road Blocks

EXTERNAL: _____

_____

INTERNAL (Current script): _____

_____

DEVELOP:

ACTION STEPS RESP.	PLAN DATE	ACTUAL DATE	ACTUAL DATE
1			
2			
3			

ENGAGE: Stakeholders in Your Support System

_____

OUTLINE: The Reason Why You Want to (Must) Make This Change?

_____

❏ ❏ ❏

Chapter 4

Identify External and Internal Roadblocks: The Second Step

We can chart our future clearly and wisely only when we know the path which has led to the present.

- Adlai Stevenson

Happiness is when what you think, what you say, and what you do are in harmony.

- Mahatma Gandhi

In this chapter, we deal with internal and external causes of life imbalance. It is important to recognize how the external demands of our work and environment affect our choices and the outcomes of our decisions. It is equally important to recognize how our internal beliefs and thought processes affect the way we respond to external pressures and how we perceive what "must" be done. The key to attaining a better life balance is recognizing and managing both internal and external causes of life imbalance.

In our day-to-day lives, we all wear multiple hats — working professional, parent, spouse, sibling, son/daughter, friend, sports player, spiritual seeker, social club member...

the list goes on. Over time, we've developed scripts for each of our roles, as to how they should be played. These scripts are a product of our education, our upbringing, the families we grew with, the larger environment we're living in, the media, and our life experiences connecting all of these.

> We're the screen writers, actors and directors of our roles in life. If we don't like how certain roles are playing out, we have to change the script. Lasting balance starts inside-out. First we have to understand what our current script is.

Most of us are slaves of the stories we unconsciously tell ourselves about our lives. Freedom begins the moment we become conscious of the plot line we are living and, with this insight, recognize that we can step into another story altogether. Our experiences of life quite literally are defined by our assumptions. We make up stories about the world and to a great degree live out their plots. What our lives are like, then, depends on the **scripts** *we consciously or, more likely, unconsciously have adopted.*

- Carol Pearson, Ph.D.
The Hero Within: Six Archetypes We Live By

External Root Causes of Life Imbalance

Causes of life imbalance may be identified as external when they involve material, physical or emotional demands originating outside ourselves. The following are common examples of such causes:

1. Long daily commute to and from work.

2. Work culture and managerial practices.

3. Work profile demanding 16-hour days.

4. Dual career/single parenting demands — not enough hours in the day.

5. Work at home not evenly shared — gender-role demands.

6. Pressure from family, society, media to succeed in various parameters.

7. Lack of training in delegation, prioritization and time management.

8. Lack of training in the Balanced Life Model of decision making.

1. Long daily commute to and from work

In all my work-life balance conversations and workshops in India, whether in Bangalore, Mumbai, Pune, Gurgaon, or any other city, one universally voiced concern was long commutes, exceeding 1-2 hours each way. Adding the commute time to the hours committed to the workplace doesn't leave much time for anything else. Furthermore, a long commute leaves people physically and mentally drained by the time they reach home.

In all major cities, rising real estate prices and lack of affordable housing are forcing people to move further and further away from their workplaces. Sometimes, even in cases where the distance traveled is only a few kilometers, traffic congestion makes it a long commute in terms of time.

2. Office culture and managerial practices

During my trips to India over the last couple of years, I've been interviewing people in various cities about their work-life balance journey and challenges. Anita, a finance professional, shared that she feels pressured to stay back in the office after work hours because her boss and co-workers are also still there, even though she herself is always on time with her projects and doesn't need to work extended hours to stay on top of her assignments. She is compelled to stay because her manager doesn't like it if associates leave before him. The manager's wife is not working and is therefore available at home to look after the children and household, but Anita's husband Anil also works full time and they have two young children. This situation creates a lot of stress.

I've spoken with several senior managers at TCS, Wipro, Infosys, Times of India, Aditya Birla Group, Syntel and other reputed organizations. When I ask them my favorite question, "What keeps you awake at night?" the response always is that "to grow and compete in today's fast changing global economy we need to innovate. We need to engage everyone in the innovation process." The unfortunately common managerial behavior witnessed in Anita's scenario is not conducive to creating the innovation culture that the senior management of her company wants. Chapter IX, 'Enterprise Growth, Creativity and Balance: The Three Legged Stool' discusses this in detail.

3. Work profile demanding 16-hour days

Take your basic 24-hour day. Subtract 16 hours for work, and you're left with exactly 8 hours to get the recommended 6-8 hours' sleep, eat three meals, bathe and dress, manage and maintain your home, and spend "quality time" with your family. You don't need a calculator to conclude that the numbers simply don't add up!

The solution to this predicament is quite simple. Either find another planet that has 48-hours in a day, or find a job that demands fewer hours. Most professionals will agree that, locating a planet with 48-hour days would be easier than coming to grips with the painful reality of their work schedules.

Where does the 16-hour day come from? Sometimes it comes from bosses or managers who put in long days at work themselves and start expecting the same from subordinate employees. These individuals typically measure their personal success solely in terms of earnings or corporate status, and allocate their time accordingly.

When this definition of success is imposed on employees and co-workers, taking time for self, leisure, and relationships may be perceived as an act of corporate treason!

Long days are also common in the fields like teaching, social services, counseling, government, medicine, etc. Professionals in these fields are "helpers" who serve human needs on a daily basis. Because the need is often greater than the resources available, the urge to spend some extra time or to do "just one more thing before leaving" is almost overwhelming.

Where does a teacher draw the line, knowing that many students might not pass without after-school tutoring? How can the Human Resource Director decide to call it a day when facing a distraught employee who has appeared just two minutes before the end of office hours? How does a physician get any rest when an elderly patient refuses to acknowledge a holiday because "Nobody else can take care of me the way you do"?

Corporate greed is not the only cause of the 16-hour day. Reasonable requests from reasonable people can snowball into a 16-hour day just as easily as unreasonable requests from overambitious bosses.

A subtler and insidious source of the 16-hour day is cultural expectation. The executive who is seen mowing his lawn or the physician who volunteers to be P.T.A. president is likely to become suspect. Executives and professionals are just somehow "supposed" to be at the office from 8 to 5 (or 6, or 8 or 10!). Cultural stereotypes abound, encouraging overwork at the office and inattention to life balance.

The author and co-author represent both the corporate and human services fields. It is our experience that the 16-hour day can be created just as easily in one setting as the other. The effects of putting in these days are remarkably similar across professions. Spouses and children come to feel "less worthy" than the office. Professional contributions grow stale. Health problems gradually begin to crop up. Make no mistake – the 16-hour day does not come cheap. It exacts a heavy price.

4. Dual career/single parenting demands — not enough hours in the day.

For many of us, our parents did not prepare us for the world in which we now find ourselves. It is not that they were intentionally neglectful. They simply could not train us for something they never experienced.

Fathers who fulfilled the traditional "provider" role were not expected also to be adept at being actively engaged in children's activities, communicating and sharing household responsibilities. Mothers who were full-time homemakers did not have to "steal time" from work to attend the kindergarten play.

Instead of adapting or modifying the roles we saw our parents perform, most of us have simply added more roles to an already challenging job. Unfortunately, taking up more roles and responsibilities does not add more hours to our day. We work hard and we work 'smart,' yet, we often feel unsuccessful, frustrated, resentful, and overworked.

Amanda and Neal:

Amanda and Neal put every minute of their time to use. Their friends marveled at how productive they were. They both worked full-time during the week and made time to help their children with homework and after-school activities. As there was no time for household work during the weekdays, Amanda and Neal used their weekends to cook for the coming week and to do the laundry and housework. Their job responsibilities were fulfilled capably; their house was clean; their meals were nutritious; and their children received plenty of "quality time." Yet, Amanda and Neal felt exhausted, unable to understand why they often felt incomplete and had no time left for each other.

Trying to play multiple roles has an interesting effect on us (besides exhaustion, of course). While our opportunities for success are multiplied, so are the chances of failure. On one hand, working parents have the opportunity to be successful in their career, parenting, homemaking, time management, and leadership. On the other hand, they also face a risk of failing at each of these tasks. It is very tempting to focus only on the failures!

Guilt and frustrated expectations seem to fall especially heavily on working women. Modern dads can change a few diapers, run a carpool occasionally, and in just a few hours per week they might even exceed the role models they grew up with! Women who were reared by full-time homemakers can devote 40-50 hours per week to their children in addition to work responsibilities and yet, not even meet the expectations with which they were raised.

> Women who were reared by full-time homemakers can devote 40-50 hours per week to their children in addition to work responsibilities and yet, not even meet the expectations with which they were raised.

In these situations, our perception of what constitutes success and failure can be more relevant than the actual physical and mental demands of our roles. Our perception of what is necessary determines how many tasks we take on, and the measure of success or failure that we feel at the end of the day.

Male or female, no working parent can get everything done alone. Those who try to conquer these challenges alone are chronically frustrated and bitter. Only those survive, who learn three important skills:

- Expecting and receiving help from family, friends and paid workers
- Delegating authority
- Setting priorities

These skills are essential for any working parent, and form a key to surviving the challenge of tackling these responsibilities successfully.

5. Work at home not evenly shared - gender-role demands

If evolution really works, how come mothers only have two hands?

- Milton Berle

Today, such a clear and simple division of cultural roles and responsibilities exists in only a small minority of American families. Economic and social changes have been so dramatic that the modern family is hard-pressed to keep up in terms of developing viable family roles and equitable divisions of labor.

Division of labor at home continues to be a problem in even the most progressive and "liberated" households. Studies of two-career families indicate that women continue to perform well more than half of all household and child-rearing tasks regardless of their financial or professional status vis-à-vis their partners.

This situation creates problems for both sexes. Men who are actively involved in home and child care could do twice as much as their professional peers, and yet only half as much as their spouses would like! The dilemma for women is often that of competing professionally with men who are able to use their after-work hours for professional reading or "power golf" rather than laundry, meal-preparation and carpooling.

The tasks that are associated with the female-role stereotype - cooking, cleaning, shopping, child care, etc. - cannot be ignored. They are necessities of life. They can also become a bitter battleground between spouses. The time spent arguing over whose job it is to do the laundry could be better spent in working out creative solutions for getting it done. Consider the following:

SALLY: "When my first husband and I divorced, I taught my daughter to do laundry. Now that I am remarried, we continue to be responsible for our own laundry, and my husband does his alo."

MEG: "During times when I am unusually busy at work, we eat out. The kids love it, and I save not only meal-preparation time but grocery shopping, planning and clean-up time."

During the height of the post-World War II "baby boom," if a father could change a few diapers, attend the school play, and grill the occasional weekend steak —he had pretty well fulfilled his family responsibilities. 'Balanced life' consisted of making time to play golf on weekends, reading The Wall Street Journal, and taking the wife out to dinner. During this same period, women performed most of the homemaking responsibilities and had few personal or cultural pressures for career accomplishments outside the home. Gender roles were clear, and responsibilities were divided accordingly.

DAVE: "Our children each cook dinner one night per week — even the 9-year-old. Not all our meals would make the cover of Good Housekeeping, but I have more quality time with my children in the evening, and they are learning independence as well as cooking skills."

> Test your own creativity with this exercise: In one minute, list all possible methods of feeding a family of four an evening meal five nights per week.

If you came up with only two or three possibilities, you probably need some more practice in creative problem-solving. If you came up with six or more, you're well on your way to turning an age-old conflict into a creative growth opportunity.

6. Pressure from family, society, and media to succeed.

The pressure can be as subtle as a friend or relative bragging on the success of a mutual acquaintance, or as direct as a child's innocent question, "Why don't we have a swimming pool like the Mitchells?"

Pressure to succeed is now finding its way into the preschool and kindergarten. Entrance exams and I.Q. tests for 2-and 3-year-old preschoolers are no longer uncommon in the higher-priced private schools, despite adequate evidence that such tests are unreliable during the early years.

> Pressure to be successful comes from all directions — family, friends, co-workers, the media. Even the words we hear during childhood echo in our ears as we strive for success in the adult world.

A magazine article I recently came across described what clothes and toys parents should buy their 5-year-olds to prepare them to take the kindergarten entrance tests. We are forcing children into a success/failure mode before they even have the opportunity to develop their talents and find out what they do well.

The problem with any measure of success — from first-grade report cards to annual profit-and-loss statements — is that no single measure fits everyone. The executive who is a good "idea person" may be a poor "detail person." The well-rounded college student may lack the impressive GPA of the devoted bookworm. A good team player may not be the one to score the winning touchdown.

You can no more measure creativity with a College Board score than you can measure a person's weight with a yardstick. It just doesn't work. A wise educator once reminded the parents of her gifted students that when they entered the business world, they would not be "ability grouped." They would be expected to know how to work with all kinds of people, to bring out the best in others, and to show leadership in groups of people with diverse talents, skills, and backgrounds. She knew that her students needed more than high achievement-test scores in order to be successful in life.

> The danger we face as adults is in using someone else's yardstick to measure our own success. To do so is a prescription for frustration and failure.

Our friends may measure their success in ways that may or may not be relevant to our own lives, be it number of promotions, salary, golf handicap, frequent-flyer miles, or something else.

The unrealistic feelings that are ingrained in us from a young age – that we need to have massive amounts of money to be considered a success – not only leads us to a higher likelihood of feeling inadequate, anxious or depressed, but also makes us think that the only value in getting an education is to make a lot of money, which is the wrong way to look at it.

**A 21-year old student at the
University of Miami**

7. Lack of proper training in the use of delegation, prioritizing and time management

Ask any successful business person or professional about the skills that are critical to effective performance and you will almost always find delegation, prioritizing and time management on their list.

Look at any educational curriculum for a business or professional degree, and you will somehow find a peculiar absence of those same skills! If we assume that these critical skills are not a matter of genetic inheritance, then we may also assume that each of us enters the workplace lacking some of the tools that are critical to success. Many businesses and professional organizations offer excellent continuing education and professional-development seminars on time management and other leadership skills. Such programs focus more on practical application of these critical skills at the workplace, and do not expand the notion of management or leadership to a 24-hour day or whole-life model. The problem is that we are in fact, whole people who don't turn into someone radically different during the hours we spend at work.

Leadership begins at home. Professionals who are not able to manage their 24-hour day will have more difficulty in managing their work than someone who exhibits effective leadership in all aspects of life.

Unfortunately, there are even fewer formal trainings or learning opportunities for whole-life leadership than there are for the specific skills of prioritizing, delegation, and time management. Another (and closely related) external root cause of life imbalance is lack of training and experience in the Balanced Life Model for decision making.

8. Lack of training in the Balanced Life Model for decision-making.

Balanced life is a lot like marriage and parenting — two very important jobs for which we have virtually no training to start with! To complicate matters, the balanced life skills we may have observed in our parents and mentors in the past may not be adequate for the situations we face today.

The holistic Balanced Life Model includes career development, health and leisure skills, personal relationship building, self-actualization, and spiritual growth. If we learn these skills at all, they are likely to come in bits and pieces: a career-development seminar at work, a marriage or parenting workshop in the community, or a weekend spiritual retreat at one's preferred place of worship. Nowhere do we have the opportunity to take our lives as a 'whole' and develop the skills to address the big picture.

Dave:

Dave was an executive in retail management who found himself unable to handle even mild confrontations with his employees, despite having superior skills in other areas. The problem was that his personal, career, leisure, and self-fulfillment needs were all wrapped around the job. His friends, social activities, and self-esteem were all dependent on his job and co-workers. He was reluctant to confront co-workers who were also friends, and his job performance was suffering as a result.

Dave had received training in all the management skills, including conflict-resolution training. However, the skill he needed most as a manager was unknown to him. If he had been as skilled at managing his life as he was in balancing a budget, Dave would have known that having all of his personal needs tied to his work was a risk not only to his personal well-being but to his work performance as well.

In Dave's situation, the solution to his problems with conflict resolution was actually to be found outside the workplace. Once he was able to develop relationships and interests outside the workplace, conflicts at work became less threatening, and he was able to apply his conflict-management skills more effectively.

This approach to decision-making is leadership at its best.

In the Balanced Life Model, leadership begins at home, and good management begins with having an overall plan or mission for our own lives, that includes our work, our relationships, our health and leisure, and our self-actualization and spiritual growth.

> The holistic approach of the Balanced Life Model may be compared to an effective long-range corporate development strategy. Each decision is evaluated in terms of its contribution to the overall mission of the organization as well as its immediate result or outcome.

Internal Root Causes of Life Imbalance

Internal causes of life imbalance involve our own thinking, feelings and perception. How we react or respond to an external stimulus, such as a demand on our time, depends a great deal on our internal belief system, our script.

1. More work hours mean more success

2. I'm doing it for them

3. Work, the only source of fulfillment

4. The busier I'm, the more important I'm

5. Must stay connected 24/7 otherwise I'll miss out on...

6. Avoidance: Busy lifestyle provides shield from personal issues

7. My needs come last

8. Successful life = More money than others

9. I can/must have it all

10. I can and must do it all

11. Unclear life goals and priorities

1. Hours = Commitment = Promotion (Career success)

It seems the corporate world projects this message that an employee putting in more hours is more committed. At times they may even reward this behavior with a promotion, which then becomes the employees' script. As we discuss it further in chapter IX, 'Creativity: The Key to Enterprise Growth and Career Success,' this script serves neither the organization nor the employees well.

2. I'm doing it for them (my children)

One of the comments I get often during workshops and executive coaching is, "Madan, I'm doing it for them (my children)!" Of course, we all want our children to be happy and to provide the very best we can for them.. We don't merely wish them to be happy while they're at home, but also be prepared for a productive, meaningful and balanced life after they take the proverbial flight from their nest. To do this, we try to provide a good education, a loving environment at home, and by supporting their choice of extra-curricular activities. A greater role in this process is played not by our lectures but by our examples. If the President of the United States can make time for sharing experiences with his daughters, surely we can too.

Obama says being President has made him a better father

Michelle and I can go to parent-teacher conferences together. I've been able to make Malia's tennis matches and Sasha's dance recitals. Sasha let me help coach her basketball team – the Vipers. They won the title. I've even experienced what all dads dread: watching my daughter go to her first prom in high heels.

**Jan 12, 2016, Robert Baldwin III,
The Huffington Post**

One of the most important things we want to give them is self-confidence. The confidence in themselves to solve the problems they're going to face in life. That inner confidence is developed when their 'I matter' needs are met. How do they know that they matter to the most important people - their parents? Children feel that when parents are present to share their accomplishments, joys, and even disappointments. Just being around, building memories (taking pictures or videos) of moments turns them into shared experiences.

"My husband never took time to understand their school problems or personal problems when they were little, and when it meant a lot for dad to care. Now they don't come to him, and he feels hurt and angry. He says he has given them so much and they are ungrateful. They just don't feel they can really talk with him now."

From the Wall Street Journal series, "Executives' Wives Describe Effects of Husbands' Careers on Children," - As told by a wife in her 50s

3. Work, the only source of fulfillment

Another frequent comment in my workshops is, "Madan, I love my job. I enjoy working long hours." When people say this, I tell them that "It's great that you love your job, because frankly, it would be very stressful to do a job you hate. Think of your job as a dessert. Most people like desserts, but what would happen if we ate only desserts for breakfast, lunch and dinner? It may be enjoyable in the short term but will certainly lead to health issues in the long term. Similarly, work meets the needs of our career self but not of the people, actualizing and leisure selves." The next three root causes provide some insight into how work becomes the only source of fulfillment.

4. The busier I am, the more important I am

When we say to a friend, "Man, I'd love to join you for the cricket match but I'm just swamped at work," the ego feels good about it.

"The busier we are, the more important we seem to ourselves and, we imagine, to others. To be unavailable to our friends and families, to be unable to find time for the sunset (or even to know the sun has set), to whiz through our obligations without time for a single mindful breath – this has become the model of successful life."

"Sabbath: Remembering the Sacred Rhythm of Rest and Delight,"

Wayne Muller,
Bantam Books, New York

Ego makes the person feel that he or she is irreplaceable.

One of the hardest things to accept is that we are replaceable. Intellectually, I think we all know it. But it's harder to accept it emotionally. And, to a certain extent, you feel like saying, 'But wait a minute, how can things be continued without me?'

Eliot Spitzer, April 27, 2009, Newsweek

5. Must stay connected 24/7, otherwise I'll miss out on ...

According to a survey by Oxygen Media, 37 percent of women respondents aged 18 to 34, agreed to have fallen asleep with a smartphone in their hands. This was back in 2010. Recent studies show that for a much higher number of people, the last thing they do before going to bed and the first thing they do after waking up, is to check their smartphones.

"Now with e-mail and with the advent of the BlackBerries and hyper-accessibility, there is this sense that if you don't show that you're always prepared and ready to respond and address an issue, then somehow you're going to be perceived as not being conscientious or not keeping up on things."

Tom Britt, Professor of Social Psychology, Clemson University

On a flight to New York I was sitting next to a man in his thirties who was busy with his phone for most of the journey. I asked him, "Why are people these days always occupied with their smartphones?" He responded that, "There is a sort of high you experience when you see something new on the screen." Later when I read the following, I fully understood what he meant.

Just as cigarettes came to be viewed as nicotine delivery systems, mobile computers and phones may really be neurotransmitter delivery devices... This neurotransmitter-addiction theory helps explain a lot of mobile phone behavior, including the universal tendency for people getting into elevators to check their e-mail, despite having just checked it, oh, 45 seconds before.

Lee Gomes, Senior Editor, Forbes

6. Avoidance: Busy lifestyle shields from personal issues

It is easy to avoid thinking about our lives by staying in constant motion. If there's one word that seems to characterize the current generation best, it is "busy." This constant motion appears to be a function of external causes — the demands of career, family, finances, social obligations, etc. However, it is actually an internal curse.

No one forces us to take on all these commitments. At some point, we chose each one ourselves. This can be a shocking revelation for many of us. It's a sobering exercise to think backward to the point in time when we actually chose to take on each of the commitments that may now seem to be more burden than challenge: marriage, jobs, running a home, completing graduate school, church participation, civic leadership, raising children, traveling, friendships, etc.

How does a once joyful choice become a burden? The problem lies not in the quality of the choice but in the method of choosing. No one taught us how to make choices, readjust priorities and adapt our lives to ever-changing economic and social realities. Instead, we choose everything that comes our way and lose ourselves in the maddening dash to keep up with all of it.

> Like a circus juggler we end up having so many objects in motion that we cannot move ourselves. We are rooted where we stand by the fear that one bad move or minor lapse of attention will bring everything crashing down on us.

"The vicious cycle continues as we become so busy trying to fulfill all the commitments we have that there is no time left to think about where our lives are going. Maintaining a complicated life is a great way to avoid changing it."

Elaine St. James, quoted by Michael Warshaw in Fast Company

Those of us who remember watching a circus know that even the most skilled juggler has to stop somewhere and collect all the objects he's been juggling before he can move on to the next act. He simply cannot start a new routine until he has finished the old one. He carefully collects all the balls, plates or pins, refocuses his attention and begins the next act by tossing up new objects into the air one by one until he has reached the maximum number he can manage.

Like the juggler, we must stop every now and then to evaluate whether we are to be able to do anything except standing in one place, juggling the same commitments. Reflection is necessary for growth. The avoidance of reflection created by a too busy lifestyle is ultimately self-defeating.

Effort without purpose and direction becomes meaningless and unproductive. We may do so much and yet find ourselves without any sense of accomplishment because we didn't know where we were headed in the first place!

It is especially important to take the time to stop and reflect on our lives as wholes — work, relationships, leisure and fulfillment. There's nothing wrong with being busy as long as there's a sense of purpose to the effort.

7. My needs come last

During my interview with Beverly, a freelance designer, I asked, "How do you find time for yourself?" She responded that, "it's kind of a female thing I think to be so selfless, to give your all, to fulfill this person's needs and that person's needs, and do this and do that, and suddenly you discover you've been drained dry and there are no reserves left! That just adds

> "It's kind of a female thing I think to be so selfless, to give your all, to fulfill this person's needs and that person's needs, and do this and do that, and suddenly you discover you've been drained dry and there are no reserves left!

to the problems. Having some time to myself has really been a good thing. I regret that I didn't demand it before, because I now feel that it would have been good for my marriage. I would have had a much better outlook, and been a much happier person if I just had a little time to myself to be able to regain my reserves."

Women put too many expectations on themselves: having a career, being physically fit, being in good relationships with family and friends, reading good literature, doing community work, recycling and buying green, and involved in some sort of spiritual quest. And when they fail to accomplish all that in one day, they go to sleep thinking, 'I didn't get done what I needed to, and somehow that is my fault.'

Mary Pipher,
Author, Speaker, Psychologist

8. Successful life, i.e. more money than others

At some point in life (often during middle age), adults become acutely aware of time. Not only are there too few hours in the day, suddenly one feels that there aren't enough years in which to accomplish all the dreams of youth.

This awareness typically strikes home in two ways: negative comparisons with peers or relatives; and negative comparisons with one's own expectations, dreams, or fantasies.

The author's personal experiences have confirmed for him that negative comparisons with others' success create anxiety and a chronic sense of dissatisfaction, no matter how impressive and long the list of one's own personal achievements is.

I look forward to visiting relatives in India. It is a pleasure to attend the weddings, and a joy to meet nieces and nephews and see how they have grown since the last visit. Most of the relatives on both sides of the family have done well for themselves financially. The one inescapable part of the visits I could do without are the conversations with the more affluent relatives regarding how someone else has netted a "bigger deal" than them. As the conversation progresses, it becomes more and more obvious that comparing accomplishments in this manner is preventing them from feeling good about their own achievements in life.

Because we live in a competitive world, it is normal for us to feel some anxiety in evaluating our accomplishments against someone else's definition of success. The issue here is how we deal with it. Do we deal with it in a healthy or unhealthy way? Do we stay depressed? Do we continue to feel anxious? How long do we take to snap out of these negative feelings?

One reaction to the bad feelings engendered by these comparisons is to "pick up the pace." Becoming a workaholic might mask our insecurities, but doesn't heal them. Developing broader and more appropriate personal goals for a balanced life — the big picture — is far more likely to result in a genuine, healthy and lasting sense of satisfaction.

On the way back from a family vacation in Hawaii, I stopped in San Francisco to visit a very close friend. Ashok and I started our careers at the same time. Looking at his home and his position at work, it was obvious that he was earning more than I was. On the flight home, the difference I perceived between his success and mine started to nag me, resulting in feelings of anxiety and dissatisfaction.

My experience prompted me to take a paper napkin and draw the Balanced Life Model on it to answer my main question, "Am I getting what I want out of my life?" Thankfully, the results were both pleasing and surprising to me: Career Self — a career which challenges me, helps me grow, and in which I enjoy the respect of colleagues and superiors; People Self —

a lovely wife, two healthy children, ample time to be part of their activities, and a good circle of friends; Actualizing Self — a lifestyle which allows enough time to devote to reading and writing, conduct workshops about balanced living at nearby universities, practicing my faith and nurturing spiritual development; Leisure Self — playing tennis twice a week with friends I love to meet, leisurely walks around the neighborhood with my wife several times a week. The C-PAL exercise enabled me to evaluate my own bottom line (not someone else's!) and to realize that what someone else has achieved is of little relevance to my own life.

We look around and find many "models" of success in practice: prestige, money, houses, cars, vacations, corporate success, sales figures, social engagements, and even children's accomplishments.

The other problem in using someone else's model of success is that there will always be someone who "has more" or is "doing better." Only by developing and using our own model of success, can we come up with life goals and activities that fit us so perfectly that absolutely no one could "do it better."

> The problem with accepting or internalizing someone else's measure of success is that it simply may not fit you. Like a set of clothes borrowed from a stranger, someone else's model of success may not fit your unique combination of talents, abilities, and resources.

9. I can/must "have it all"

We are all bombarded by the marketing message, "You can have it all." After hearing it repeatedly, we internalize it and tell ourselves, "I must have it all!" This message can be a positive motivator only as long as "all" is defined very, very carefully. The list that makes up "all" must be a strictly individual matter, and every item on the list may not be achieved simultaneously!

Operating under the belief system of "I must have it all," we wear ourselves out by running after every piece that make up the picture of "all" in our minds. A media woven dream picture of "all" includes a successful career, regular promotions, a happy marriage, a luxurious home, multiple cars, impressive vacations, a circle of attractive friends, well-adjusted children who star in sports and make the honor roll, a Garden Club yard of the month, participation in social and civic organizations, a beach-worthy physique, etc.

Reality however, is sobering. The economy; a fiercely competitive work environment; only 24 hours in the day; the early years required for building a career often being in the same time period in which our children grow up; the aging human body, etc. All of these factors get in the way of "having it all," especially all at once.

Usually we look at people who are financially successful and assume they must "have it all." If we really knew all about that person's life, we might see a very different story.

An individual may be successful materially, and yet not feel secure or even financially successful. Personal or family health may not be in the best shape; relationships may not be prospering; or there simply may not be any time to enjoy the fruits of hard-earned success. The appearance of "having it all" doesn't help one escape reality.

10. I can/must "do it all"

The companion to "having it all" is "doing it all" — the pitfalls of which are evident in the following personal account from the co-author:

One lovely morning in May, it happened: My child finished a nutritious breakfast without complaint, the baby-sitter arrived promptly, the beds were made, lunch and supper menus were prepared, my business suit was pressed and clean, my briefcase was filled with completed work, I had a stimulating conversation with my husband over breakfast and I left for work on time! Feeling content and fulfilled, I pulled out of the driveway, marveling at how clever I had been to manage it all. Like King Arthur and his knights, I had created the perfect environment — my own Camelot!

It would be at least six months, however, before I experienced Camelot again. Within one week, the baby-sitter had been called away to tend to a sick relative, my daughter had developed a fixation on nutrition-free cereals, my briefcase was bulging with unfinished work, my house was buried under a mountain of dust and laundry and four crisis- laden days in a row had left my husband with no time or energy for relaxed conversation. My own sense of contentment vanished just as quickly as it had come.

"Doing it all" was often held up as the ultimate achievement for women of the Eighties. What many of us found was that doing it all:

- Results in fatigue, which dulls the sense of accomplishment

- Cannot be sustained over a long period

When we are too tired and frustrated from trying to "do it all," we feel chronically behind and frustrated no matter how much we achieve. Our many worthy successes are summarily sacrificed on the funeral pyre of our failures.

The Camelot story affects men in a different way. Reared on personal and media role models of corporate success and little in the way of home responsibilities, they are now coming home to wives who have been at work all day. Both partners tend to arrive home late, tired and preoccupied, wishing desperately that the "dinner fairy" would appear and put a hot meal on the table. Men too are often pressured to "do it all" without slowing their climb up the corporate ladder. What about Camelot? Is it necessary to

> Stress-related illnesses, career burnout, substance abuse and family conflict are among the prices paid for trying to do it all.

give up dreams in order to develop workable roles and goals? Is it possible for one person to actually enjoy his or her career, family and personal life? It is not necessary to give up dreams, but a few dream-management strategies are necessary to bridge the gap between fiction and reality.

Here is the sequel to the co-author's Camelot story:

I have become better at sequencing and prioritizing roles. I can do it all — but not all at the same time! I ask for help and receive it. I accept my children's version of a cooked meal or a clean room in exchange for not having to do it myself. I have become willing to pay more attention to my successes than to my failures. Life in the real world can be fun and fulfilling without perfection. I've also learnt to enjoy those "brief shining moments" when it all comes together. I now know those moments won't last forever, but I also know they'll surely visit again.

The past repeats itself only because a person makes a present choice from what is contained in his or her memory bank.

- Terry Cole Whitaker

11. Unclear life goals and priorities

Without clearly defined life goals, we have no sound basis for making choices regarding how and where to spend our limited time and energy or look beyond today. Only we can define the right goals and priorities for us at any stage in life. To get started, the short exercise in the previous chapter posed two questions. "What are we after in life?" The most common answer to this is 'happiness.' The second question: "Looking back over the past year what are the things/experiences/activities that made you happy?" The answer tells us what we need to do more for us and our loved ones to be happy.

We certainly have more than one year of life experiences at our disposal. By processing life experiences we gain insight into the deeper question, "What really matters?" Socrates said that, "An examined life is not worth living. And, it is the hardest thing you'll ever do." Why is it hard? Because the examination might reveal things that may make us uncomfortable, such as learning that the most important things in life aren't 'things' at all! Or the goals we're pursuing do not reflect our true priorities. It may ask to change our script and priorities. We all know how uncomfortable change is, don't we? Escaping introspection and change is the ticket to avoiding facing yourself and your problems. We can try but the problems and stresses created by unfulfilled work-life balance needs won't simply go away.

Finally, some scripts are conscious while others live in the unconscious. The interesting thing is that unconscious scripts can drive our choices without us being aware of their existence. The question we need to ask is that, "is this script supporting me in my goal of enjoying a balanced life journey, full of love and laughter, or coercing me into making choices leading to an unbalanced life journey?"

Practical Application Example
Enjoying Life Today and Building Memories (V.I.D.E.O.) for Tomorrow

Personal Action Plan

Celebrating Life in its Fullness, One Week at a Time

NAME : *Madan Birla (Dual Career Couple, Daughter 8, Son 13)*

WEEK OF : *March 2*

VISUALIZE: A Balanced Week and Choose One Activity You're Not Doing Now

Attend both Children's Talent Shows and after School Games and Recitals

IDENTIFY : Internal and External Road Blocks

EXTERNAL : *Meeting Conflicts at Work*

INTERNAL (Current script) : *Hours = Commitment = Promotion*

If I Take Time Out for Personal Life, I May be Short Changing My Career Advancement Potential and the Company Itself (Fedex) I'm Doing it for Them

DEVELOP: Action Steps To Overcome The Roadblocks

ACTION STEPS RESP.	PLAN DATE	ACTUAL DATE	ACTUAL DATE
1			
2			
3			

ENGAGE: Stakeholders in Your Support System

OUTLINE: The Reason Why You Want to (Must) Make This Change?

❑ ❑ ❑

Chapter 5

Developing Action Steps to Overcome the Roadblocks: The Third Step

Today well lived makes every yesterday a dream of happiness and every tomorrow a vision of hope. Look well, therefore, to this day.

- Kalidas, an Indian poet of the 4th or 5th century

To live in the present does not imply rashness or irresponsibility or selfishness; it is not an act of hedonism or of cowardly escape. It is to live with instant appreciation of the good in life and in freedom from obsessive anxiety.

— Charles Morgan

We drift into a way of life and may never find out until it is too late that it wasn't the kind of life we wanted. This happens when we follow the "Psychology of More"

- "I'll spend more time with the family after I receive this promotion."

- "We'll be happy when we buy that flat."

- "If I can get just one more contract, I will have it made and I can quit worrying about the credit card payment."

When we live for tomorrow, the present eludes us.

This chapter will present specific ideas and tools to help you develop a personal balanced-life action plan that allows time for career, relationships, leisure and actualizing activities in a balanced manner on a weekly basis, if not on a daily basis.

Invariably, the root causes of life imbalance reflect a combination of the internal as well as the external. The solution will involve dealing with both — changes in values within to address the internal root causes, as well as relationships with the outer world to address the external root causes.

CAUTION: Do not try to use all of these ideas at once! Go back to Chapter 3 on Root Causes of Life Imbalance and identify the most important causes of imbalance in your own life. Then select the practical ideas that will help you most effectively address the sources of imbalance.

> Intellectual understanding without action will not result in changes needed to regain the balanced life. Action without understanding results in shallow or short-lived change. Both have to be addressed. One won't work without the other.

Each idea has a "think" and a "do" component to help you address both internal and external issues as you develop your own plan. Finally, enjoy your own creativity and add your own ideas to the list.

While working on this chapter, I sent letters to 40 well-known successful people, from various fields - business, politics, media, and, sports. My one-page letter requested them to share one strategy/idea which has helped them balance their lives. I heard back from Bill Clinton, Robert Schuller, Helen Gurley Brown, Sam Walton, Lou Holtz, Fred Rogers, Tom Harkins, Mary Kay Ash, Lynn Martin, and Monty Hall.

1. Reclaiming your life one day at a time — making your calendar work for you

Think... of your calendar as representing your life, not just your list of work obligations, appointments and commitments to others

Do... Schedule the People, Actualizing and Leisure activities first on the monthly calendar before scheduling business appointments and career activities.

I remember being one of the few fathers at the school talent shows. The joy shared at these moments cannot be described in words. I look at the conflict between work and family in these situations as follows: If I can find the time to be with my child when she or he is sick, surely I can find time to share his or her joyous moments. Most of us in the professional ranks are paid for the quality of our decisions/work and not by the hour. We can include family and personal time in our work day.

"When I was taping my show at NBC Burbank, I left between shows to attend my son's Little League games some 10 miles away. It meant so much to him to see his father in the stands. I do the same today for my grandson. I never missed my daughter's plays or recitals. As busy as we are, there is still time to invest in your family. As a result, we are as close today as our family could be."

— **Monty Hall**
TV Game Show Host

2. Share your balanced life priorities and action plans with people in your life

Think... of how it is a wrong assumption to believe that you know what your significant other's and children's' priorities are. Ask them, "Are my priorities in synchronization with yours?" Even if you knew what these were a year ago, they change as people grow. Balanced-life plans must be regularly updated and discussed with those close to you.

Do... allow others to remind you of your balanced-life plan! Once you have told your children that the family will be going somewhere for the weekend, they won't let you forget that. With all the demands on our time, it is good to have someone reminding us of our own balanced-life plans.

3. Say 'No' to requests and activities in conflict with your balanced-life plans

I am criminally well-organized and I prioritize (what a dreadful word!). Friends, husband, job, sex, family... all the important things I fit in. Peripheral stuff that has to be taken care of — the house, Christmas presents for people who help you all year long, dental, doctor, hairdressing — I also fit in. Since I like work so much better than play — for me work is play — I don't have to worry about tennis, sun-bathing, racquetball, rock-climbing, etc. There are plenty of other things I don't fit in that people pester you to do. I am able to say "no" ruthlessly. We're back to my first thoughts — organization and prioritization (gracious, how dull!) are the only things that allow balance in life."

— Helen Gurley Brown
Cosmopolitan Magazine

Think... about the message here. Unless we watch what we obligate ourselves to do, we can easily lose our life balance. Don't try to be everything socially that's not you.

Do... evaluate each request on your time and energy in terms of your personal goals and balanced-life plans.

4. Be continually aware of the blessings in life

Think... about how the success gap is such a powerful negative force waiting to disturb the life balance, especially in successful and achievement-oriented people. We tend to take the most valuable things in life — health, love of family, supportive friends, evening walks, successful projects/accomplishments at work — for granted. Taking stock and being aware provides a solid foundation and the right attitude to successfully deal with the problems.

To remember that who we are and what we become has its roots in our childhood. To know that what is essential is invisible to the eye. To believe that the Creator of the Universe cares about each one of us in a unique and loving way

— Fred Rogers
Mr. Rogers Neighborhood

Do... start each day by taking a moment to reflect on something or someone for which you are thankful. If you tend to forget the positives, write them down in your calendar, diary or journal.

5. Do things for people less fortunate than you

Think... about the world beyond your home and office walls... about your place in the universe rather than your position in the office... about what you have to share with others and what others have shared with you

Do... things for people who are less fortunate than you are. There are so many such people, and you will be amazed at the positive effects you experience.

"Visit a hospital, homeless shelter, and it makes me realize that I am fortunate to have my problems, because with God's help I can solve them. This works for me whether I'm on a roll or depressed."

— Lou Holtz
Former Head Coach, University of Notre Dame

This helps us in the action plan discussed in Number 4 above. We all write checks for United Way, American Cancer Society and other charitable organizations. But there is a special joy in doing things firsthand and reaching out to others in person.

6. Minimize financial worries by living within your means

Think... about how credit cards, equity loans and store financing make it easy to buy this and replace that. Living from paycheck to paycheck creates a tremendous sense of financial insecurity and creates tension in relationships. Both conditions impact balanced life in a very negative way.

I experienced this feeling when I was laid off from my first job after only three months. Fortunately, I was able to get another job within a month. But since then, I've saved and put away funds for covering all home expenses for at least a year. I remember a friend who within a month of losing his job saw his wife leave him, too. The pile of bills and no income was just too much stress for the relationship to handle.

Do... learn how to make choices. Discuss those choices and teach your children how to make them as well. (As in: We can eat out twice a week or we can take turns cooking at home and save the money for that trip we've all been wanting).

7. Use the balanced-life model's C-PAL circle to remind and reinforce the balanced lifestyle and to counteract 'make it' pressures

Think... about your whole life and not just your job.

The focus point of my life is my daughter and wife. I derive my strength and enthusiasm for my work from their love and encouragement. When I place my family first and everything else behind them, then I am able to maintain my life balance.

— President Bill Clinton

Do... draw the C-PAL circle on a piece of paper every six months or so and review each of the components to make sure your current lifestyle is celebrating life in its fullness.

8. Notecard exercise: An excellent tool for enhancing relationships on and off the job

Think... about how we tend to assume that family, friends and co-workers automatically know what you appreciate about them. In our busy lifestyle, we do not take time to tell each other the good things.

Do... get the family or work group together and pass out a clean sheet of paper to each member. Ask each person to complete the following sentence: "I like you or I appreciate you because..." for everyone in the group including himself or herself. After everyone is finished writing, each person reads aloud her or his compliments. If there are six persons in a group, then each member gets to hear six beautiful compliments.

Collect all the sheets and have each person's compliments typed on a blank note card. You can carry a card in your briefcase and read them whenever you need a lift.

9. Share experiences and not just things

Think... about the last time you shared an important experience with someone close to you. Remember that gifts are no substitute for shared experiences.

You wanted to know how I maintain a balance between my professional and personal life. I must tell you that time with my family is vital to me. Although it is sometimes difficult, I make it a point to spend as much time as possible with my wife and two daughters. In fact, I make it a point to be with my family on our birthdays and holidays, regardless of my professional schedule.

— Tom Harkins
United States Senator

A few years back on a flight from Memphis to Las Vegas, I was sitting next to a high school teacher from Las Vegas. Conversation revealed that the teacher and his family were returning to Las Vegas after visiting the New Orleans World Fair. During a discussion on balanced-life issues, he shared his philosophy.

He said, "I have a daughter in high school, and we try to do as many things as we can as a family. To afford trips like this on a teacher's salary, it means continuing to drive and repair my old car. I believe it is more important to share experiences than things."

Do... look on your calendar and see if you have each member of your family listed by name at least once this month. Even something as simple as "read a book to Suzie," or "watch Mark's new break-dance routine" will help you make time to share experiences.

10. So what if it takes 10 years to learn and/or get into something you would really like to do?

Think... about walking a mile one step at a time. How many times during the course of a year do you hear someone or even yourself say, "Oh, how I wish I could do that," or "What I'd really like to do is..."?

One solution to this kind of thinking came in Dr. Crawford's career counseling class:

"If you get started today, you'll be there two years from now. Otherwise you'll still be saying the same thing next year and the year after that." In our instant gratification culture, it is very difficult to have that much patience. However, because the average life span is now more than 70 years, we do have the opportunity for more than one career.

As a matter of fact, the seeds for this book were sown 10 years ago when one of the authors enrolled in a counseling degree program while working as a manager! Although we don't exactly know the path that life will take over a 10-year period, if we get started, there is a good chance that we'll get there. Goals leading to self-actualization are worth the effort, because in the process we discover and celebrate who we really are.

Do... identify a small step toward one of your life goals and start working on it today.

11. Allow time for developing and expressing your spiritual dimension

Think... about your values. Your spirituality may involve prayer, meditation, nature or other activities. Do not assume that spirituality is reserved only for those who belong to churches or organized religious groups. Spirituality is a part of each human being. In order for life to be whole, all the pieces must be there. Otherwise, there is a vacuum.

> Although we don't exactly know the path that life will take over a 10-year period, if we get started, there is a good chance that we'll get there.

I suspect if proper balance in life is to be maintained, there should be a standard of high moral values at all times, respect for family, church affiliation, work enjoyment, and community involvement.

— Sam Walton
Founder of Wal-Mart

Do... find others with whom you can share and discuss your values. Put your values into practice. Notice the values that are reflected in your calendar and your checkbook.

12. Enjoy the moment: Do fun things today

Think... about the following comments made by a participant after attending the Leadership and Balanced Life seminar: "A tiny delicate flower may seem insignificant by itself but can color a hillside in sufficient numbers. Small pleasures and rewards can add up to fulfillment if repeated."

Do... make plans and share them with others.

In my family, it is a must that we have a family activity every week in which the whole family participates: movie, play, miniature golf, bowling, picnic, outing, etc. Although my teenage son would often try to get out of it, it was him who reminded me this summer (before he went away to college) that it was time to renew our family subscription to Theater Memphis.

13. Keep your life values and priorities in focus all the time

Before founding Mary Kay Cosmetics, I had over 25 years' experience in the direct selling field. In working with women, I found that the most important things in their lives were their faiths and their families, with their careers taking third place. After retiring in 1963, I decide to start my own company, hoping to give women a work opportunity that would offer them a chance to keep their priorities in the proper order. Our company philosophy became and remains today — "God first, family second, career third." Our Beauty Consultants work the hours they choose. Today our sales force is nearing a quarter of a million, and it has been said we have more women earning over $50,000 and even $100,000 a year than any other company in America. Our top people can earn this kind of money and still keep their lives in balance!

— Mary Kay Ash
Founder, Mary Kay Cosmetics

14. Develop and use your faith

Think... of how spiritual faith provides the foundation for optimism. Thirty years ago I saw the following quote at an Art Fair, hand written on cloth by an artist. It got my attention and has been hanging on the sink since then. I can't help but read it every morning while brushing my teeth.

All that I have seen teaches me to trust the Creator for all that I have not seen.

Do... discriminate between what you can and cannot control. If it is helpful, make a list of your worries, then separate it into what you can and cannot control. Use your spiritual and faith development to let go of what you cannot control.

15. Talk out your worries

Think... how lack of time and energy — the two personal resources — stops us from leading balanced lifestyles. Worrying saps more energy than physical exertion.

> Psychological studies have shown that optimistic people with talent do better than pessimistic people with similar talent.

Do... acknowledge personal problems. This is difficult for individuals who have always relied on their independence. Talking to a trusted friend or a relative can help you sort things out. Men especially need to guard against thinking, "I'm not supposed to have self-doubts."

16. Avoid irritating and overly competitive people

Think... of how we tell our kids to be careful about the type of company they keep because we are concerned about their being influenced negatively — drugs, alcohol, anti-social behavior, etc. Yet even we as grown ups are influenced by the kind of company we keep. Overly competitive people always want to win at work and often even at play. Competing in everything and with everybody is not conducive to building relationships.

Do... pay attention to your personal "barometers" that tell you if the company you are keeping is enhancing your life or detracting from it. When the social party debates become heated and personal, the party that was supposed to be a light and fun evening leaves you mad and drained. Limit your contact with people and situations that leave you feeling drained, tense or irritated.

17. Take time to talk to yourself for learning from the greatest teacher: Life

Think... of how psychologists once said that if you talked to yourself you were not 'OK' mentally. Now we know that to stay in touch with ourselves, we need to have some inner dialogue

Do... ask, "Am I getting out of life what I want?" Also, we need to listen to the unmet needs of the different dimensions of the self. This requires us to be still periodically, as the outside and the inner "noise" can drown out this small voice.

18. Take time to pamper yourself

Think... about how you feel when you do take time (even for just a few minutes) for yourself. Consider the following conversation with the spouse of a successful executive:

After I send the kids to school, I go to my husband's office. In the evening, I cook, clean and put the kids to bed. Weekends are busy with soccer games, shopping... I just don't have time to do anything myself.

Q. How does that make you feel?

A. Resentful at times.

Q. Are you a better person to be around when you are not resentful?

A. Of course I am!

Do... put time for yourself on your calendar and give it priority!

19. Delegate, delegate, trust, trust

Think... about the fact that one of the key skills of a successful manager is delegation. In reality, most managers under-delegate and thus overload themselves. Since there are only 24 hours in a day, the extra hours taken for work have to come out of the other three components: People, Actualization and Leisure.

Do... delegate tasks at work. It is not only good life balance, it is good management

The experience of learning over the years to delegate and then seeing the results and then delegating more and seeing the results and really building a good team around you, where you are in a position where you're not trying to do their job for them because they don't want you trying to do their job for them. They shouldn't be there if you don't have total confidence in their ability to do the job.

Somebody asked me a question a couple weeks ago at a social function. We had been talking a bit about what we did for a living — you know, who we work for and what our jobs were and all that other stuff, and they said "How in the world do you stay on top? You've got 90,000 people... blah blah blah... How do you sleep at night?"

I said, "I sleep like a baby." They looked at me like "Huh?" and I repeated, "I sleep like a baby." Then I explained, "The Senior Vice Presidents that we have at our company — I'm speaking especially

about my group, but they are all the same way — are absolute top-notch. They're doing a terrific job, and on a day-to-day basis I never worry about what are they doing out there to screw up. It doesn't enter my mind because I know that they are very proactive, are making the right kind of decisions and the right things happen. I do — I sleep like a baby.

If through reports and conversation I see a trend that may concern me or something like that, then I'll pick up the phone and say, "What's going on? There is something here that I want to know about and etc., etc." Frankly, those are pretty few and far in between.

— Bill Razzouk
Executive Vice President, FedEx

Do... delegate tasks at home. It is not only good life balance, it is good parenting!

A busy physician and father of four commented about his children's rooms: "Of course, they are not as neat as I would keep them. The point is that they are learning responsibility, and I am not spending my valuable family time putting away toys!"

20. The weekly schedule must include some time for just the two of you

From the start of my marriage, my wife, Arvella, and myself have made the commitment to have a weekly date night with each other. Every Monday night is reserved on my calendar for her. When the children were young, we left them with a baby-sitter. Now that all five of our children are grown and married, they have adapted "date night" into their lives as well.

— Robert Schuller

21. Sequence

Think... about what you want to accomplish over your lifetime, rather than what you want to cram into the next few weeks. Consider that you may not be able to achieve all your goals simultaneously, but may be able to attain most of them during your lifetime.

We cannot give top priority to everything at once. Yet most of us do not relish the idea of having to choose between family and career. One way out of this dilemma is to sequence priorities:

- Delaying starting a family to devote time to career;

- Slowing down the career track when children are young;

- Putting in overtime in order to have a three-day weekend;

- Adding more household help during peak workloads;

- Reducing expenditures in order to reduce overtime and increase family time;

- Buying a new house and driving an old car;

- Driving a new car and keeping the old house;

- Skipping the vacation this year to save for the big trip next year.

Sequencing priorities is critically important in the lives of women, who are vulnerable to feeling chronically torn between home and career.

In my early 20s, my fantasy was to have a house, a Ph.D., a Mercedes-Benz and a baby. The car came first — a used foreign car was manageable on two incomes and no children! The Ph.D. came next, but was interrupted by the arrival of our first child. By the time the Ph.D. was finished, the foreign car was gone, replaced by an unpaid student loan and a family station wagon. Later came home ownership and another child. Looking back, it all worked out well — just not all at the same time!

— Cecilia Marshall

Do... keep your priorities before you. Write them down if necessary. Evaluate them regularly and change them when needed.

22. Take occasional unplanned long weekends

Think... always that creativity is the key to keeping relationships (the People component) alive.

Do... be creative in finding destinations within the town where you live or within a four hour drive.

23. Use the C-PAL circle to evaluate and focus on the changing needs of people in your life

Think... about how all things in nature want to grow. If a tree is not growing, it is dead.

Each member of the family has the same four needs as you do, but the content and proportion of those needs change over time. The 'People'self in a 5-year-old needs the constant assurance of parents that she or he is somebody to somebody. When the child becomes a teenager, the peers occupy a larger role in the desire to be somebody to somebody. It is not that teenagers truly want to make parents' lives miserable. But painful conflicts often arise as they attempt to meet their changing "I want to be somebody" needs.

Do... listen to the balanced-life needs of others in your family. Do discuss how you can encourage and enjoy each other's growth rather than being threatened by it.

24. Give yourself positive strokes/rewards for leading a balanced life — because the outside world does not

Think... of how a balanced life provides its own rewards and its own reinforcement. The pulls in the media and environment are toward leading an unbalanced life. By giving ourselves positive strokes, we strengthen the inner core and are less negatively influenced by the external forces.

Do... Reward yourself with mental recognition, books, movies, a chess game, a concert, spiritual retreat. Spend time with other people who share your values and exchange positive strokes. Read books that support and reinforce your values and spiritual commitments.

25. Re-evaluate your goals

Think... that if you are tormented by unrealized career and material goals, you need to evaluate the goals to see if they are realistic and achievable.

The reality of the corporate world is that there is less and less listen to the balanced-life needs of others in your family. Do discuss how you can encourage and enjoy each other's growth rather than being threatened by it.

room at the higher levels of the organizational pyramid. You may have the necessary skills and desire to be the vice president or president of the company; but it may not be achievable if the incumbent is not going to move.

It is good to have goals, as long as they are a source of positive motivation. However, if the reality of economics or competition is making them unreachable, we need to step back and reassess the situation.

In a recent seminar on connections between work and family, there were several family counselors present. They commented that they are seeing more and more people suffering with the ill effects of the "making it" pressures. These are people who are successful in other people's eyes, but have not yet achieved the higher goals they set for themselves.

Do... use the C-PAL Circle as a tool to help you maintain (or regain) your sense of proportion.

26. Have a place for retreat at home — workshop, garden, study, etc.

Think... of the human need to get away from the pressures of "being somebody." The word "recreation" literally means "to be created again." This is how we feel when we are refreshed by a hobby or creative outlet, a new idea gained from reading or a change of pace.

The C-PAL Circle reminds us to look at the career as one part of this multidimensional life, versus letting life be completely dominated by career.

Refinishing furniture: getting dirty and messy is a great relief — the product of one's own hands is always better.

Lynn Martin
Former U.S. Secretary of Labor

Do... something!

27. Use all your vacation days

One hears often in the corporate world: "I have not taken a vacation in so many years." She or he may think that he is doing the company a favor by not taking the allowed vacations. In reality, the company may be losing out on the employee's creative input.

Also, vacations with family and friends help by sharing experiences. Not all vacation days have to be used for long or out-of-town trips. I get four weeks' vacation. Two weeks are planned as family trips out of town. The other two, I just take one or two days at a time. Some days I schedule when schools are closed for one day holidays. Since my wife has just started a new job, she does not get four weeks. So on such days, I just plan a day in town with my daughter and her friends. On our last such outing, we went to Pizza Hut for lunch and then to the bowling alley. These are the girls I have known since they were 2 years old. It is just a sheer joy to see how delightful and interesting these young ladies have become. To share this joy, one just has to be around to listen and observe.

Also, on some vacation days, I just spend the whole day at the library to catch up on magazine articles.

Think... of the fact that you have earned those vacation days. They are yours. So use them — if only for one-day outings.

Do... use these days off to share yourself with the loved ones. Use these days to do the things you love to do but can't find the time — even if it means doing nothing!

> Vacations play a very important role. Time off from work recharges the battery and helps clean the cobwebs so creative ideas do become accessible.

28. Stop and look at the family photos in the office

Think ... Most of us have pictures of our families in the office. In the drive to empty the In-basket, there is not much free time left. In the drive to accomplish, it is easy to forget who we are working so hard for. When you are busy, the time just flies.

The trouble comes when years just fly, and before you know it the little boy is taller than you are. We need something and somebody to remind us that there are things for which we just take time out now because they won't be available later.

The family pictures in the office are waiting to remind us that this little boy or girl is growing up fast. We need to share and assist in important events before they are all grown up.

Do... stop and look at the family pictures and notice how fast the kids are growing. If you keep reflecting on that regularly, then it won't be hard to leave the office for two hours in the middle of the day to be at the school play or the piano recital.

29. Loosen up on the cleanliness standard

Think ... For most families, middle-class status is achieved by having two incomes. The demands of the day job, raising children and maintaining the household does not leave much time or energy for anything else. In this environment it is essential that you loosen up on the cleanliness standard for the house. Trying to maintain an absolutely clean house drains energy and uses up precious time.

Do... loosen up on the cleanliness standard and use that small amount of free time for taking a walk (L), going to a movie with a friend (P), reading the book you've been wanting to read (L), or playing with the kids (P, L).

30. Use the drive time to and from work to concentrate on what is important

The key to minimizing the briefcase of office work with you in the evening is to complete the important work while at the office. So on the drive to work, in addition to making a mental list of the "to-do" items, also reflect on what you're not going to waste your time on — the unimportant things.

Use the drive from office to home in the evening to concentrate on what is important when you get home. What is important in the evening is to acknowledge everyone in the home with a smile as you walk through the garage door.

It is through everyday behavior that we tell people what is really important to us. Of course, it is the people in our life! But if the work worries are creating an environment for the people in your life to wonder what mood you'll be in today, it is time to take some action.

31. Clear communication with the significant other

Angie and Craig both have successful careers and two preschool children. Angie was feeling resentful because she felt that Craig was not doing his part in helping with the children and the homework. The problem, as she described it, she had been expecting Craig to read her mind. Now she writes down her expectations and communicates clearly the tasks on which she needs Craig's help.

32. Use the lunch hour for running errands

Do ... Make a list of your errands and use the lunch hour to run as many errands as you can. This will free up time after work in the evening and on weekends to spend with family or for doing things you like to do.

> Remembering what you did right, versus focusing on what you could have done better or did not get to, helps put a smile on your face as you walk through the door.

33. Use technology

After the birth of her first child, Swati, a management consultant, bought a home computer with a modem connected to her company's computer. This allowed her to work from home, and she demonstrated to her supervisors that she was equally productive there. She scheduled two half days at the office each week for face-to-face interaction. The flexibility she gained was worth the investment.

In the information economy, most professionals can do a good part of their job from home with the use of personal computers and fax machines. Most corporations do not want to lose the expertise and experience their people have, and are open to these arrangements.

34. Reduce trips to the supermarket

To make sure all the needed items are bought during the weekly trip to the supermarket, Cathy has computerized the grocery list. A copy is posted on the refrigerator. Everyone in the family circles the items as they are used up and need to be replenished

35. We cannot do all things — so hire help

One of the things I admire in America is the interest and the ability of people to fix things around the house. But as we assume more responsibility at work, and family obligations increase, there simply is not enough time to do everything. This "to-do" overload can cut into People and Leisure time. One solution is to hire help for some of the routine chores.

36. Less time in the kitchen

Sam and Denise do their weekly cooking on Sunday afternoons for the whole week. Some dishes are cooked completely, while others are cooked partially. This way, whoever gets home first can get started toward having the dinner ready. Some days they pick up a dish from the deli or the health-food store.

37. Keeping romance alive

Next Friday, ask your significant other to meet you for lunch. Give sufficient notice so that he or she can make arrangements to get away for the afternoon. Before leaving your office for lunch write down on a blank card the five things you like about him or her.

After lunch, catch an afternoon movie. After the movie, share a cup of coffee and conversation or a stroll by the lake or through the park.

You may be saying to yourself that you cannot leave the office and "waste time" like this. Trust me, the business will not shut down because you are only going to put in 56 hours this week instead of the regular 60 hours. Suppose you were coming down with the flu — you could leave the office for the afternoon then, couldn't you?

The best use of time in life is the time we waste on people we love.

38. Say aloud: "It is important to me"

You may have noticed by now that many of the practical ideas discussed here are fairly simple. The challenge is to put them into practice in your life. As discussed many times so far in the book the key to a successful balanced-life effort is the internal resolve to say to yourself: "It is important to me, and I am going to take time to do this."

39. Read and reflect on spiritual material every day

Even if it is only for five minutes a day, the benefit in terms of internal strength and peace will be far greater than from anything else you could do in five minutes. You will have access to more of your inner resources and learn from the wisdom of the spiritually enlightened souls through their writings.

40. Ask regularly: "Am I getting out of life what I want?"

How much fulfillment or enjoyment we get out of life is the direct result of how we are living our life. So if we are not getting out of life what we want, then we need to examine how we are living our life and identify the changes we need to make.

41. Use the power of positive thinking and speaking

Our mind's search engine operates like a computer and acts on the request received. If I want to like you then my mind looks for the reasons to like you. If I decide that I don't like you then my mind will give me all the reasons not to like you. Visualize and think out loud the desired state.

"She loves me because I love her (unconditionally)."

"I'm enjoying a balanced life because I make time for fun with family."

"My friends understand me and make time for me because I make time for them."

• • •

Balance conversations in India

While in Pune to conduct the 'Enjoying a Balanced Life' workshop, I had a chance to spend time and converse with Karen Anand. Karen has been described as the 'Martha Stewart of India' and a 'food guru', influencing the way people eat and perceive good food in India. In addition to writing extensively on food and wine for almost 25 years, she has also built her own brand of gourmet food products, run a successful chain of food stores, created a niche catering business, anchored top rated TV shows, and started a Gourmet Academy., Karen also consults for various multinationals companies, and International hotel and restaurant chains, and still manages to find time to cook!

> I believe that through our thoughts, we don't just send instructions to our minds but to the universe. Positive thinking and speaking helps create favorable conditions for our goals and relationships.

Q. Karen, How would you define a successful life?

"For me, I think it will be a combination of some level of financial success to lead a comfortable lifestyle, a close and supportive family, and the opportunity to pursue my passion. I've been fortunate to achieve this combination. Professionally, the opportunity to work in different areas and be creative has been very satisfying. Looking back, I think a sense of accomplishment would be an important component of a successful life."

Karen is the founder of the hugely successful Farmers Markets by Karen Anand, a whole foods food and drink fair, which began in Pune in December 2012 and has now expanded to 7 Indian cities. She also oversees a line of gourmet products under the Pune Farmers' Market brand. Relentless, she has returned to her first love, food and travel writing, a passion that takes her around the world, as she reports and reflects with depth, complexity, generosity, and great style!

Q. What strategy/idea has helped you maintain life balance?

"First, to work from home was a conscious decision. So when the kids came home from school, I'd take a break to be with them. I know how critical this flexibility was to me when my kids were young, so I make sure my staff has the same flexibility. Moving out of Mumbai (to Pune) also helped. Has it always been easy to maintain the balance? No. But, I believe that with conscious effort and planning it's possible to enjoy both, a successful career, and a fulfilling family life."

The value of family traditions:

Conversation with Ravi Talwar, a successful entrepreneur, Mumbai

When asked to share 'one strategy/idea you used to maintain work/life balance,' Ravi told me something he learnt from his father - having dinner together. "Even now when my children are all grown up and have their own families, we make sure that we all meet every Sunday for lunch. And, during the summer we all go on a holiday trip together."

Ravi developed a proprietary technology for gluing flexible packaging material used in products ranging from Maggi to pan masala, to potato chips and innumerable other products. He set up a factory in Navi Mumbai so he could be home in time for dinner with his family. Realizing the importance of work/life balance, he was one of the first business owners in India to implement a five-day week policy for his employees in 1984.

I grew up in New Delhi and my happiest childhood memories are with my family, celebrating Holi, Diwali, Raksha Bandhan, Durga Puja, Dussehra, and other festivals. Here in the U.S., my son lives in New York and daughter in Chicago. But, we've always made sure to get together on Diwali, and to take a weeklong summer holiday trip every year. We've added Christmas to our list of get-together occasions.

"Whatever your family might look like, taking the time to create or honor a family tradition is well worth the effort. When the toys have lost their charm and the clothes are out of style, we'll remember those moments and the love that made them happen."

**Barry Ebert,
Science of Mind, December 2008**

There is no "perfect" balance, and no one is able to sustain the balance over the long periods. But the effort itself will make the journey more enjoyable.

Do not try to change everything overnight. Just pick out one idea or activity and implement it for at least two weeks. Then pick out and implement another idea. Take your time.

Practical Application Example

Personal Action Plan

Celebrating Life in its Fullness, One Week at a Time

NAME: *Madan Birla (Dual Career Couple, Daughter 8, Son 13)*

WEEK OF: *March 2*

VISUALIZE : A Balanced Week and Choose One Activity You're Not Doing Now

Attend both Children's Talent Shows and after School Games and Activities

IDENTIFY: Internal And External Roadblocks

EXTERNAL : *Meeting Conflicts at Work*

_____

_____

_____

INTERNAL (Current script): Hours = Commitment = Promotion

If I Take Time Out for Personal Life, I May be Short Changing My Career Advancement Potential and the Company Itself (Fedex)

I'm doing it for them

_____

_____

_____

_____

DEVELOP: Action Steps to Overcome the Roadblocks

ACTION STEPS	RESP.	PLAN DATE	ACTUAL DATE
1. Revise the script As a planning director I'm paid for the quality and creativity of my decisions and not by the hour. Also, as leader of 30 people my most value added contribution is to create the environment for each professional to excel and help them become the best they're capable of becoming. By taking time for a fulfilling family life I'm more creative and effective leader at work.	MB	Feb. 16	Feb. 16
2. Ask children 2 weeks in advance about upcoming games and recitals	MB/ Kids	Feb. 16	Feb. 17
3. Turn the work calendar into life calendar. Meet with Carol.	MB/ CA	Feb. 17	Feb. 18

ENGAGE: Stakeholders in Your Support System

_____

_____

OUTLINE: The Reason Why You Want to (Must) Make This Change?

_____

_____

❏ ❏ ❏

Chapter 6

Engage Stakeholders in Your Implementation Support System: The Fourth Step

During a Balance workshop in India, Arun asked me, "Madan, when we know what the right thing to do is, why don't we just do it?" I posed Arun's question back to the rest of the class and received the following responses.

- We are creatures of habit and it's more comfortable to stay with what we're used to than make a change.

- There is a strong psychological payoff for continuing our bad habits.

- We have limited time and energy so we do what seems urgent at any given moment.

- We have a strong built-in preference for instant gratification.

- Procrastination comes easy to us – e.g. "I'll start exercising/dieting tomorrow."

- Reinforcement from the media to focus more on material/career success.

To build the implementation support system, share your goal and plans with other stakeholders - spouse, children, a close friend, boss, secretary, as suitable, and ask for their help.

When I was at FedEx, a senior vice president once shared with me a copy of the work-life balance contract he had signed with his kids. He kept a framed copy of this contract on his nightstand and asked them to hold him accountable. The children did their part by reminding him whenever he got too busy to spend time with

> Change is hard to make, even for a good cause. Our chances of successfully making a change are much greater if we have a strong support system and a partner with mutual accountability.

them. Merely having a balanced life plan is of no value unless the new habits are integrated into our day-to-day lives. Studies have shown that long term health benefits come from making incremental, sustainable changes to one's lifestyle.

We all know that we should eat less and exercise more, but we often miss the mark. We can always benefit from a nudge. In addition to helping us build a support system, this step provides several other benefits, all of which are very helpful in constructing and enjoying a healthy and fulfilling lifestyle.

1. Building the much needed implementation support system

2. Understanding each other's 'script'

3. Meeting stakeholders' 'I matter' needs by asking for help

4. Not expecting others to read our minds

5. Learning about ourselves from others

1. Building the much needed implementation support system

Practical application example:

As you'll notice in my V.I.D.E.O. planner, my children and secretary are the key stakeholders that play a part in implementing the steps necessary for my goal of attending my children's talent shows and after school activities. The children supply information about their upcoming activities – games, recitals, etc. The secretary is in-charge of my calendar, i.e., scheduling meetings and controlling what gets on the calendar.

After getting activity information from the children I would review with them my plans of attending their games and recitals. By doing this I created expectations and made them my accountability partners. Having this information on the calendar allowed my secretary to plan my meetings and appointments around the children's activities as much as possible. Since most of the activities were after normal working hours, there wasn't much conflict. She made sure I left the office in time to attend the kids' activities. Did I always make it to all of their activities? No, but I'd say being present 80% of the time is not that bad.

Personal Action Plan

Celebrating Life in its Fullness, One Week at a Time

NAME : *Madan Birla (Dual Career Couple, Daughter 8, Son 13)*

WEEK OF: *March 2*

VISUALIZE: A Balanced Week and Choose One Activity You're Not Doing Now

Attend both Children's Talent Shows and after School Games and Recitals

IDENTIFY : Internal and External Road Blocks

EXTERNAL : Hours = Commitment = Promotion

If I Take Time Out for Personal Life, I May be Short Changing My Career Advancement Potential and The Company Itself (Fedex)

Current Script: I'm Doing it for Them

DEVELOP : Action Steps to Overcome the Roadblocks

ACTION STEPS	RESP.	PLAN DATE	ACTUAL DATE
1. Revise the script As a planning director I'm paid for the quality and creativity of my decisions and not by the hour. Also, as a leader of 30 people my most valuable contribution is to create an environment for each professional to excel and help them become the best they're capable of becoming. By taking time for a fulfilling family life I'm a more creative and effective leader at work.	MB	Feb. 16	Feb. 16
2. Ask children 2 weeks in advance about upcoming games and recitals	MB/ Kids	Feb. 16	Feb. 17

3. Turn the work calendar into a life calendar. Meet with Carol.	MB/CA	Feb. 17	Feb. 18

ENGAGE: Stakeholders in Your Implementation Support System

While Reviewing the Week and Month Ahead Every Monday Morning with Carol, My Secretary, Make Sure the Children's Talent Shows and Games are Marked on My Calendar.

OUTLINE: The Reason Why You want to (Must) Make This Change?

People want to get into exercising but they don't have the discipline. Invite a co-worker to take daily walks with you. Join a walking group. We change best when we change together.

Zac Sims, age 30, began meeting personal trainer Kelly Wight of Envision Memphis twice a week last November. He has lost 75 pounds and is going to run his first 5K. Advice: Find someone to keep you accountable – your wife, your best friend – someone you can look in the eye and someone you fear disappointing."

**Healthy Living, The Commercial Appeal,
October 3, 2011**

2. Understanding each other's script

Life has taught us that love does not consist in gazing at each other but in looking outward in the same direction.

- Antoine de Saint-Exupery

During the height of the dot com phenomenon, I was invited to speak at a Tech Conference in Silicon Valley. My message was that "to build a lasting business in today's fast changing global economy, you need to provide lasting leadership, i.e., you need to be around not just physically but also creatively. You need to provide creative leadership to continually adapt to a changing environment. Working 24/7 is possible but inevitably leads to a burnout in a few years. This way, you won't be the creative leader your organization needs you to be. Therefore, balance must be an integral part of your equation for building a lasting and successful business."

After the talk Susan – one of the attendees - approached me and requested that I meet with Mike, her boss. I told her that I was flying back to Memphis the following afternoon. She insisted - "Please have lunch with him on your way to the airport. I'll clear his calendar." I asked, "Why do you want me to meet with him?" She said, "Mike and his wife are expecting their first child and I literally have to push him out of the office at 10 pm every night. His life is completely unbalanced."

The next day, I met Mike for lunch and brought up his secretary's concern about the lack of balance in his life. Mike sighed and said, "You know, women just don't understand."

I said, "I'm not sure what you mean by that. What is it that women don't understand?"

He clarified, "Now is the time to make money in the tech business. So, I'm looking at this whole balance thing on a four to five-year horizon. My wife talks about balance every week."

I responded, "Mike, in our leadership class at FedEx a question we always ask is, 'What's the one thing a leader must have before he or she can truly lead? People answer, 'honesty, trust, technical know how, passion, etc.' but the right answer is 'willing followers'. By himself, a leader cannot accomplish much.

"The next question we ask is, 'Why would people follow you?' Because people share your vision, they like where you're going and want to be part of it.

"Similarly, a thriving relationship needs a shared vision. I'm not saying that your vision is wrong or your wife's vision is right. Next weekend when both of you are relaxing in the backyard, ask her about her expectations from you and your role after the baby arrives. Listen carefully, and then share your vision and plans. Then develop a common vision - a script for the relationship going forward."

In some parts of our lives men and women have different scripts. According to a small study released by the British research and consulting firm, MindLab International, a successful shopping session can produce a euphoric experience equivalent to kissing and other romantic experiences.

"That's perfectly normal. For a man to stand in line for a book about 'How to lead a balanced life,' first he would have to acknowledge that there is a problem. Remember, we are a species that doesn't like to ask for directions even when we know we're lost!"

Following a book signing at People Soft's user conference in Los Angeles, I was having lunch with Jack, an old friend. I shared with him that, "yesterday, I must've signed over 200 copies of my 'Balanced Life' book. One peculiar thing I noticed was that over 90% of the people who lined up to get a copy of the book were women who asked me to sign it for their husbands."

Jack smiled as he said, "That's perfectly normal. For a man to stand in line for a book about 'How to lead a balanced life,' first he would have to acknowledge that there is a problem. Remember, we are a species that doesn't like to ask for directions even when we know we're lost!"

> People relate to people at the 'feelings' level. Being analytical all the time makes us inaccessible. The act of sharing the V.I.D.E.O. balanced life plan conveys to the stakeholder a feeling of partnership.

"Someone made me a bumper sticker that reads GOT WAKE? And I keep it with me all the time. I have this theory that your wake, just like a boat's, is much bigger than you realize. Everything you do — and what you don't do — impacts the people around you a lot more than you think."

Kip Tindell, CEO and Co-Chairman,
The Container Store

3. Meeting stakeholders' 'I matter' needs by asking for help

Men take pride in their independence and don't like to ask for help. Loved ones always want to help. Letting them help is one way to make them feel that they matter to you. Asking for help demonstrates trust and faith between you and another.

We get past the notion that we are bothering people, understanding that asking is a gift, allowing them to step into compassionate service. There is power in connecting authentically through our feelings with one another.

Science of Mind, April 2008

It tells them that making time for shared experiences is your personal priority. By sharing values and priorities you're inspiring others. Talking about how you want to spend the week helps create the life you want to build together. Initiating this conversation for seeking their help lets others share ideas you may not have considered.

> In the expression, 'I love you,' love is a verb. So, in a loving relationship each partner first needs to find out what makes the other person happy and then take action to fulfill that need.

4. Not expecting others to read our minds

For my Masters in Counseling course work, I took a class in marriage and family counseling. The professor invited a marriage and family counselor to be a guest speaker. He devoted the whole session to talking about love in the context of a relationship.

He said, "The basic definition of love is that your happiness is as important to me as mine. The complete definition of love is that your happiness is more important to me than my own." He went on to explain that in the expression, 'I love you,' love is a verb. So, in a loving relationship each partner first needs to find out what makes the other person happy and then take action to fulfill that need.

We get so busy in our daily routines, that we assume we know what makes our significant others or the children happy and take for granted that our partners know what makes us happy. By reviewing our V.I.D.E.O. planners with our loved ones, we are sharing what makes us happy and not expecting them to read our minds.

No matter how close we are to someone, we cannot expect him or her to read our minds. We may feel our inner thoughts (scripts) are clear and obvious, but that is usually not the case. Expecting our unspoken thoughts to be understood by someone else, apart from hindering the conveyance of our true feelings, is patently unfair.

**Ron Vernon, Science of Mind,
February 2006**

This is an ongoing process. Because two people who are well connected today are not going to stay the same as the years go by. Once children are born, without even realizing it we get so busy with them that spending time with each other takes a back seat. I remember reading somewhere that the best thing a father can do for his children is to love their mother. I'd like to add for balance that the best thing a mother can do for her children is also to love their father.

5. Learning about ourselves from others

After the sports section I enjoy reading the comic strips in the morning paper. Several years ago, I cut out a 'Dennis the Menace' cartoon. In this cartoon, Dennis is standing next to a guest sitting in the living room, asking him, "If you're not married, who tells you when you're doing something wrong?"

We have a natural human capacity to overlook stuff in our lives. We can easily rationalize our behavior as being right. Only others can tell us how we come across to them. Ralph Waldo Emerson said that other men are lenses through which we read our own mind.

The following joke I heard several years ago illustrates this point well.

A man was stopped on the highway by a police officer who noticed his erratic driving. The man had had too much to drink. The policeman asked the man to exit his vehicle and was talking to him when a crash took place right across the road. The officer said, "Wait right here while I go and check that crash."

Seeing an opportunity to escape, the man got into the car and drove off. He got home, parked the car in the garage and told his wife, "If someone comes looking for me tell them that I've been sick and in bed all day."

An hour later the policeman knocked on the door. When the man's wife opened the door the policeman asked, "Is your husband home?"

"Officer, he is sick and been in bed all day."

"Can I speak with him?"

The wife took the policeman upstairs to her husband.

"Didn't I see you an hour ago?" the policeman asked.

"Must be a mistake officer, I've been in bed all day."

"Can we go to your garage?"

The man took the officer down to the garage and opened the door. The policeman pointed out that the car parked in the garage was the policeman's.

The Church Health Center (CHC) provides healthcare for the working uninsured and promotes a 'healthy body and spirit' for all. For a few years I volunteered there and got to know Dr. Scott Morris - an inspiring man and the founder and executive director of CHC. He writes a healthcare column in the local newspaper. His column, titled 'It takes a village to build a healthy body' summarizes beautifully the value of a support team.

It's incredibly hard to live a healthy life all by yourself. I'm convinced that being healthy occurs only in the midst of a community. Friends, family, co-workers, and fellow seekers of the life well-lived are necessary if you are to reach your highest level of wellness.

There are some who will say that all you need is willpower — willpower to not overeat, willpower to exercise daily, willpower to avoid excesses. To them I say, "Willpower is greatly overrated."

Few of us have the innate ability to, on our own, do all that is needed to be healthy. In order to exceed, we need help. We need each other to encourage us when we fail, pick us up when we fall and walk alongside us when we are tired.

We may be able to succeed in the short term on our own, but we do the best when we work as a team. This is true in sports ranging from basketball to cycling, and it is true in the daily activities that make life fulfilling...

Human beings are social creatures, and we need other people around us when we're working to change unhealthy behaviors. Even if you can will yourself to live a healthier life, it's far more fun to enhance your life in the company of others. So let today be the first day in your journey to a healthier life and together we can celebrate the joy of living.

- Dr. Scott Morris,
The Commercial Appeal, January 25, 2010.

❑ ❑ ❑

Chapter 7

Outline the Reason Why You Want to Make This Change: The Fifth Step

By March every year, half of all new members stop going to the health club. We need help staying on track. We need to be reminded of the personal reasons that motivated us to choose this goal. Despite all the good intentions, the activities imperative for realizing the health and fitness goals are pushed out by other more pressing demands on the calendar. The comfortable old habits do not want to let go.

Question (Newsweek's Anne Underwood): Oscar Wilde once wrote, "I can resist everything except temptation." How do you learn?

Answer (Judith Beck, psychologist): "On the first day, you write on a card a list of the reasons why you want to lose weight. Note how important each reason is to you. You will read that card twice a day for a very long time to rehearse these ideas. Later when you're tempted by a chocolate-chip cookie, you can say,

Lasting change starts inside out. People who dropped kilos for personal reasons were more likely to lose weight than those driven by external forces. Writing down and regularly reading our motivations helps us stay on track.

'I want that cookie, but I would rather lose weight and be healthier, feel better, wear a size 10.' – whatever your reasons are."

Newsweek, March 19, 2007

When our son, Naveen, was two years old, Papaji (my father-in-law) visited us in Indianapolis from Calcutta. After watching us for two weeks he commented, "I see, Monday through Friday, both of you are rushing in the morning to leave for work. You come home in the evening, all tired. Then you cook, eat dinner, go to bed, and repeat the same thing the next day. On weekends you're busy mowing the grass, trimming the bushes, working in the vegetable garden, and repairing things in the house." I said, "Papaji, life is all programmed here. We don't have to think what to do." With life on auto pilot, we don't think about the medium or long term consequences of the choices we're making today.

By most estimates, lifestyle accounts for 70 percent of our life span. Our genes are responsible for the rest. Lifestyle is nothing but the end result of the hundreds of decisions (choices) – large and small – that we make every day of our lives. Living well now is like putting money in a savings account. The dividends will come later, as you age. The better you are at "saving," the richer you will be when it is time to reap the rewards.

I started writing "Chasing Life" after my first daughter was born, and my second daughter was born before the book was finished. These were life-changing events. Before becoming a father, I didn't worry much about my own mortality. Now I want to take better care of myself so I can be there for the milestones in my children's lives. I want to see their graduations and weddings. I want to be there when they have children.

I've tried to take my own advice to heart, quite literally. I have a family history of heart disease, and I learned in the course of working on "Chasing Life" that my own long-term health was not nearly optimized. I am now trying to eat better – shooting for at least seven different colored foods a day. I'm also trying to reduce the stress in my life. Both will lower my risk of developing heart disease later.

- Sanjay Gupta, M.D.,
CNN Senior Medical Correspondent

Avoid the Danger of Falling Back into Old Routines

Making many changes at the same time is just setting yourself up for failure and the resulting frustration will lead you to fall back into the old and familiar routine (rut). Clarify the importance of the chosen goal and to stay on track, ask yourself, "Why have I chosen this goal?"

Practical application example:

When someone tells himself and his family that, "The next five years will be solely devoted to my career, and after that, I'll focus on the family," there is one big problem with this statement. Time will not stand still for five years. The children are growing older and changing. The spouse is growing and changing. The persons they are and the things they enjoy today may not be the same five years from now.

An important question to ask is, "What will happen there during the five years when you are not available emotionally and physically?" The 'why I want to make this change' in my V.I.D.E.O. planner reflects a recognition of this reality.

Enjoying Life Today and Building Memories (V.I.D.E.O.) for Tomorrow

Personal Action Plan

Celebrating Life in its Fullness, One Week at a Time

NAME : *Madan Birla (Dual Career Couple, Daughter 8, Son 13)*

WEEK OF: *March 2*

VISUALIZE: A Balanced Week and Choose One Activity You're Not Doing Now

Attend both Children's Talent Shows and after School Games and Recitals

IDENTIFY : Internal and External Road Blocks

EXTERNAL : *Meeting Conflicts at Work*

INTERNAL (Current script) : Hours = Commitment = Promotion

If I Take Time Out for Personal Life, I May be Short Changing My Career Advancement Potential and The Company Itself (Fedex)

Current script: I'm doing it for them

DEVELOP : Action Steps to Overcome the Roadblocks

ACTION STEPS RESP.	PLAN DATE	ACTUAL DATE	ACTUAL DATE
1. Revise the script As a planning director I'm paid for the quality and creativity of my decisions and not by the hour. Also, as leader of 30 people my most value added contribution is to create the environment for each professional to excel and help them become the best they're capable of becoming. By taking time for a fulfilling family life I'm more creative and effective leader at work.	MB	Feb. 16	Feb. 16
2. Ask children 2 weeks in advance about upcoming games and recitals	MB/ Kids	Feb. 16	Feb. 17
3. Turn the work calendar into life calendar. Meet with Carol.	MB/CA	Feb. 17	Feb. 18

ENGAGE: Stakeholders in Your Implementation Support System

While Reviewing the Week and Month Ahead Every Monday Morning with Carol, My Secretary, Make Sure the Children's Talent Shows and Games Are Marked on My Calendar.

OUTLINE: The Reason Why You Want to (Must) Make This Change?

Before I Know it, they'll be Grown and Ready to Leave Home for College. It is Fun and Pure Joy to See them Perform and Share in their Happiness.

I'm Helping Build My Children's Inner-Security by Meeting their 'I Matter' Needs. I Want them to Grow, to Become Secure, Balanced, Productive, and Happy Individuals. I've Learned that the Best Way to do that is by Example and not by Lectures.

People change when the pain of not changing is more than the pain of changing

A good friend Vinod, as long as I've known him, had been a chain smoker. Usually during our meetings, lunch or dinner, he would light a cigarette. After noticing for a whole week that he did not smoke I asked him, "Have you quit smoking?"

"Yes, I've not smoked for a week."

"What made you do that?"

"I was at my doctor's office two weeks ago and the doctor said, 'Ramesh, do you want to see your children grow up? If yes, then you must quit smoking.'" He pulled out a card from his wallet and handed it to me. The card said, 'I want to see my children grow up' in bold letters.

"Whenever I get an urge for a cigarette, I pull out and read this card."

Getting extra implementation help from second application of 'O'

Offer yourself reward for successfully implementing balanced life choices

After you succeed in making the new behavior a habit, the joy resulting from engaging in the activity itself will be a reward. To further reinforce this behavior/choice, reward yourself even if it is as simple as buying a music CD, a book, or an ice cream cone (which is how I reward myself. I listen to music during my 30 minute treadmill exercise in the morning, at least five times a week. This is the time I get most of my creative ideas).

You Deserve It. Celebrate!

We're social animals and respond to positive reinforcement from people in our lives. I try to visit relatives in India once a year. They congratulate me on the new house, car, promotion, book publishing, and other accomplishments. No one asks, 'We've not seen you for a year. Have you been happy?' For making and implementing balance choices we have to give this reinforcement ourselves. Celebration creates positive energy and forward momentum.

Reward and reinforce

While the goal of a healthier life is a significant reward in itself, you should also reward your hard work and discipline and take pride in the positive, new attitudes that you create. Mindful motivation begins and ends with attitude, because attitude determines everything. The thoughts that you focus on, the mindset that you hold, and the mental habits that you create determine your choices, your actions, and therefore your life.

Be proud of yourself. Generate positive feelings about yourself and your ability to make a commitment and follow through. The emotional energy generated by such positive feelings will reinforce your commitment and motivation further, helping you maintain your success cycle over the long haul.

- Rita Milios, Clinical social worker
Diabetes Self-Management, March/April 2010

Collect inspirational quotes, magazine articles, and thoughts that you've jotted down

Reading is one of my favorite pastimes and whenever I see an inspiring quote/story I cut it out and file it in a folder. I've filled three manila folders with cuttings like these. Whenever I need some inspiration I just pull out one of the folders and read a few stories from it. The following are some quotes and stories selected from my folders.

It is never too late to be what you might have been.

- George Eliot

If you really want to manage your time and get stuff done, have a burning life and work purpose that is a beacon for what you do. While they are useful, the lists, the short cuts – all that stuff – pales in comparison to purpose for time management.

Dean Fuhrman, Consultant
Businessweek, August 25, 2008

There is no better way to waste time in life than to dwell on the past.

- Bonnie Dunbar, Astronaut, NASA

I believe in the power that not only allows the sun to rise but turns seeds into flowers and dreams into realities. Every time that sun comes up, I am reminded that I am given another opportunity to live my best life.

- Oprah Winfrey

I have often been asked what I thought was the secret of Buddha's smile. It is – it can only be – that he smiles at himself for searching all those years for what he already possessed.

- Paul Brunton
quoted in Zen Soup by Lawrence g. Boldt

Nothing contributes so much to tranquilize the mind as a steady purpose – a point on which the soul may fix its intellectual eye.

- Mary Wollstonecraft Shelley

When you are inspired by some great purpose, some extraordinary project, all your thoughts break their bounds. Your mind transcends limitations, your consciousness expands in every direction, and you find yourself in a new, great, and wonderful world. Dormant forces, faculties, and talents come alive, and you discover yourself to be a greater person by far than you ever dreamed yourself to be.

- Patanjali

Keep away from people who belittle your ambitions. Small people always do that, but the really great ones make you feel that you too can be great.

- Mark Twain

Live Life to the Fullest: Enjoy Every Sandwich

Since my chemotherapy treatment, I have experienced small "Zen" rushes – an arresting sense of tranquility coupled with the heightened awareness that what I am doing at that moment is exactly what I want to be doing – whether I'm sitting in a restaurant with a newspaper, reading a book in bed, cooking a meal or watching a movie with my wife. I had these moments before my diagnosis, but not as often or as easily.

Do not imagine that love to be true must be extraordinary. No, what we need in our love is the continuity to love the one we love. See how a lamp burns, by the continual consumption of little drops of oil. If there are no more of these drops in the lamp, there will be no light.

What are these drops of oil in our lamps? They are the little things of everyday life: fidelity, little words of kindness, just a little thought for others, those little acts of silence, of look and thought, of word and deed.

- Mother Teresa

- Charles Zanor
Newsweek, August 9, 2004

Life holds out a mysterious hand ... our challenge is to grasp it, and with faith, walk boldly forward.

- Siri-Dya S. Khalsa

We don't know where our gift will bear fruit, but we do know that our gift is required. All it requires is for you to listen to the impulse that arises, as it does in each and every one of us – not because it's dramatic, not because it's particularly spiritual, but just because it's yours. You are the light of the world. What permission are you waiting for before you feel as if you could offer your gift with ease and playfulness and grace? What is your gift to the family of the Earth?

**- Wayne Muller, Author of 'How, Then, Shall We Live?'
Noetic Sciences Review, Spring 1998**

If we are to leave legacies of wisdom and love and generosity … we must carry a deep commitment to our life dreams. We must dismantle our 'vertical coffins' and we must make sure that our dreams have heart and meaning.

**- Angeles Arrien,
'The Second Half of Life'**

On the day I die, I'm not going to be asking did I sell enough books, did I make enough money, I think I'm going to be asking, did I make the best use of my limited time on earth by using the gifts I've been given to the best of my ability to address the problems and concerns and issues that were within my reach; and if on balance I can answer yes to that question, then I think I can die with a sense that I did not waste my time here.

**- Palmer
Science of Mind magazine, January 2014**

Success seems to be connected with action. Successful people keep moving. They make mistakes but they don't quit.

- Conrad Hilton

Of all the forces that make for a better world, none is so powerful as hope. With hope, one can think, one can work, one can dream. If you have hope, you have everything.

You have to believe in yourself, that's the secret. Even when I was in the orphanage, when I was roaming the street trying to find enough to eat, even then I thought of myself as the greatest actor in the world.

- Charlie Chaplin

Remembering that I'll be dead soon is the most important tool I've ever encountered to help me make the big choices in life. Because almost everything – all external expectations, all pride, all fear of embarrassment or failure – these things just fall away in the face of death, leaving only what is truly important. Remembering that you are going to die is the best way I know to avoid the trap of thinking you have something to lose. You are already naked. There is no reason not to follow your heart ... Stay hungry. Stay foolish.

- Steve Jobs
Stanford Univ. commencement address, June 2005

No matter how abominable your conditions may be, try not to blame anything or anyone: history, the state, superiors, race, parents, the phase of the moon, childhood toilet training, etc.

- Joseph Brodsky, Nobel Prize Winner
Commencement at University of Michigan

I wish I could announce a major metamorphosis in myself, but change occurs slowly and in tiny increments... I try to value my accomplishments less and my friends more. Now I sometimes stop in the middle of a tumultuous day to appreciate someone's act of kindness or courage, or even do one myself.

- Janice Handler, The Wall Street Journal

A hockey career is a temporary position. A husband and father role is forever. It's that simple.

**- Wayne Gretzky,
one of the World's best ice hockey players**

People say that what we're all seeking is the meaning for life.... I think that what we're really seeking is an experience of being alive, so that our life experiences on the purely physical plane will have resonance within our innermost being and reality, so that we can actually feel the rapture of being alive.

- Joseph Campbell

As we age it's the investment in people, in friends and family, that come back to nourish us.

**Naomi Naierman in Work &
Family column by Sue Shellenbarger
The Wall Street Journal, Dec.29, 1999**

The two most difficult kinds of clients are those who spend too much and those who save too much. You need to strike a balance between living today and living for tomorrow.

After all, the point of accumulating money is to be able to live the life you want, not to sit in a small, dark room and gloat over the size of your portfolio.

**Ross Levin, Financial Planner
Mutual Funds, Sept. '99**

You don't have to see the whole staircase; just take the first step.

- Martin Luther King Jr.

❑ ❑ ❑

Chapter 8

How Balance Unleashes Creativity:
The Key to Career Success in the 21st Century

The American publisher John Wiley & Sons released the Indian edition of my book, 'FedEx Delivers: How the World's Leading Shipping Company Keeps Innovating and Outperforming the Competition,' in 2007. Since then, I've been visiting India at least once a year to speak to managers and employees of various companies in Bangalore, Hyderabad, Chennai, Mumbai, Kolkata, Pune, New Delhi, Noida, Gurgaon and Indore.

Number One need of Organizations and Senior Management

Before speaking to the management team at any organization, I request a meeting with the CEO to learn about company's growth strategy and the challenges it faces. I start the meeting by asking, "What keeps you awake at night?" I posed this question to Azim Premji at Wipro, Prashant Ranade at Syntel, Ram Ramadorai at TCS, and several other business leaders in India. They all said pretty much the same thing, that "to continue to grow in today's fast changing and highly competitive global economy, we need to innovate. We can't keep doing business the same way we've been. We need creative ideas from employees at all levels in the organization." It was not by coincidence that I received similar responses from CEOs I interviewed in the United States, Singapore, Mexico, and Russia.

A recent poll of 1,500 CEOs identified creativity as the No. 1 "leadership competency" of the future.

Newsweek, July 19, 2010

Creativity is to the marketplace what water is to life: You can have one without the other, but not for very long.

JIM BLASINGAME
The Commercial Appeal, May 21, 2012

The impact of the move to cloud computing – where servers and software are accessed via the internet rather than on local networks or personal computers – is being amplified by other trends, from automated code-writing to increased competition and falling corporate information-technology budgets.

If Tech Mahindra, Infosys Ltd., Tata Consultancy Services Ltd., Wipro Ltd., and India's other big IT outsourcing companies fail to change, the consequences for India's economy could be dire.

'Cloud' Eats Into India's Outsourcing Industry
The Wall Street Journal, Monday, July 13, 2015

Enjoying Career Success in the 21st Century

In today's highly competitive global economy, business growth depends on the ability of the company to out-think and outperform the competition. Management desperately needs creative ideas to improve products, reduce costs, and better serve its customers.

Many people believe that the way to drive innovation is to carve out a few creative people. Our view is entirely different. We need innovation from everyone.

David Whitman, CEO, Whirlpool,
"CEOs on Managing Globally," FORTUNE Magazine

"I Like the Way You Think" started Ram on a very **successful and fulfilling career journey**

A few years ago, after a speaking tour in India, I was flying back home to Memphis. Seated next to me on this long flight from Mumbai to Atlanta was Jayant Pendharkar, Global Head of Marketing for Tata Consulting Services (TCS), India's largest information technology services company. When he learned that I live in the U.S., he asked me the purpose of my India trip.

> Ideas drive growth. Ideas create competitive differentiation. Ideas are your key to enjoying a successful career in the 21st century.

I told him I gave "Leading for Innovation and Growth" talks at Infosys, Wipro, Indian School of Business, Times of India and other companies all over India as part of my book promotion tour.

He asked, "Why didn't you speak at TCS?"

I told him the talks were set up by the public relations company handling the book tour.

Jayant suggested that I should plan to speak at TCS during my next India trip. I told him, "I'm working on another book exploring career success in the business world, and part of my research involves talking to successful business executives. So, if you can arrange for me to have an hour with the CEO of

TCS, then in return I'll give you four hours during my next India trip."

A few months following this conversation I got an email from Jayant that Ram Ramadorai, CEO of TCS, would soon be in New York and available to meet with me. We scheduled a meeting at the TCS New York office.

First, I thanked Ram for taking time from his busy schedule to meet with me, then asked him to walk me through his career journey to becoming CEO of TCS.

Ram shared, "I joined TCS in 1972 as a systems analyst and programmer in their Mumbai office. In 1979 Mr. Kohli, head of TCS, asked me to go to New York. I asked him, 'What do you want me to do there?' He said, 'Ram, I like the way you think and I'm sure you'll figure it out.'"

As they say, the rest is history. Ram's creative thinking and dedication was the key to establishing TCS in the U.S. at a time when IT consulting from India was nonexistent. As a result of this successful assignment he was asked to return to India to play a bigger role at the Mumbai headquarters. He was appointed CEO of TCS in 1996. Under Ram's leadership TCS grew exponentially. With 2011 revenue of more than $10 billion, TCS is now a globally recognized leader in providing innovative information technology solutions.

As Ram did, build a reputation for thinking creatively. Then senior management will seek you out for greater responsibilities and promotion.

Generating Creative Ideas

Creativity is Using Imagination to Ask "What if?"

What if we make this change in our business strategy,

product design, manufacturing process, distribution process, billing system, accounting system...?

Creativity is the generation of novel/new ideas by:

- Connecting dots, making connections between seemingly unrelated variables.

- Imagining things in a fresh light.

- Questioning current assumptions.

We just have to provide the right conditions for the mind to engage in generating creative ideas. The amazing thing is that you don't even have to try very hard to be creative – it just happens naturally and automatically.

> We don't have to force the mind to think creatively because the nature of the mind is to think. If the mind is healthy and growing, it will produce creative ideas.

Creativity in the Business World

Creativity is the process of generating ideas – ideas that will help the enterprise become more competitive in the marketplace. Business creativity means generating ideas that improve customer experience, create new products, increase revenue/market share, or improve efficiency.

The right conditions for the mind to generate creative ideas

Generating new ideas is a process of the mind connecting "dots" (knowledge) in imaginative ways by asking "what if?" The mind requires the following four conditions to engage in the creative thinking process:

Figure 8.1.1

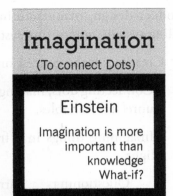

Figure 8.1.2

Figure 8.1.3

Figure 8.1.4

Figure 8.1 Four Conditions for Generating Creative Ideas

Webster's Dictionary

Mint v. To coin, to invent; to forge; to fabricate

(The mind fabricates ideas from knowledge, the raw material it has available.)

Mint n. A source of abundant supply

(The mind with its imagination capability has an unlimited capacity for generating ideas.)

The first requirement for minting or forging ideas is to gather the required raw material – more dots.

M stands for MORE DOTS: EXPANDED KNOWLEDGE BASE

Learning, curiosity, education, and creativity are part of the same constellation.

RPG, Redwood City, CA, Aug. 23, 2011, commenting online, New York Times

Creative people always ask "why?" and continually question the assumptions behind the existing business models, product designs, and business processes. These assumptions may have been valid five or ten years ago when the process or product was initially designed, but the world and technology have changed significantly since then.

Creativity is about "connecting the dots." The more dots you have to work with, the more combinations are available to help generate new ideas. Curiosity generates more knowledge ("dots"), which precedes creativity.

She was enormously curious. She wanted to know why we were doing some things at the time, and she was always prepared in a way that I thought was refreshing.

A senior Xerox executive talking about Ursula Burns, Xerox CEO, New York Times, Feb. 21, 2010

Leonardo da Vinci: A classic example of expanded knowledge base

In his August 4, 2010, New York Times column, Tom Friedman quoted Marc Tucker, the president of the National Center on Education, telling him, "One thing we know about creativity is that it typically occurs when people who have mastered two or more quite different fields use the framework in one to think afresh about the other. Intuitively, you know this is true. Leonardo da Vinci was a great artist, scientist and inventor, and each specialty nourished the other. He was a great lateral thinker. But if you spend your whole life in one silo, you will never have either the knowledge or mental agility to do synthesis, connect the dots, which is usually where the next great breakthrough is found."

I stands for IMAGINATION

Imagination is the right brain asking "what if" by connecting dots in imaginative ways, as reflected by Einstein's quote, "Imagination is more important than knowledge. Knowledge is limited. Imagination encircles the world."

At FedEx all offices had a Panaboard, a white board linked to a computer so that it could capture and save what is written on the board. Whenever someone came to my office to discuss a problem, the tendency was to start writing on the Panaboard the steps we needed to take to solve the problem. I observed that I was not alone in jumping into "how to" mode. It is a standard operating procedure for all left-brain, analytical folks. Creative problem solving requires use of both sides of our brain, the analytical and rational left and the imaginative and intuitive right. But creative thinking starts in the right brain. Using their imagination, creative problem solvers explore "what-ifs" before locking into "how to." The Disney Corporation calls it creative employees "Imagineers."

An imaginative mind borrows a technology or processes from one field and uses it to solve an unrelated problem in another field.

From NASCAR Pit to Scalloped Potato Production

For switching over from scalloped to au gratin potatoes you have to stop the line, do some cleanups, in some cases change the dimensions of the parts on the line ... In a couple of these plants (at General Mills) the changeover could take as long as 12 hours, and so you'd be down and wouldn't be getting the production during that time. Implementing ideas spurred by a team visiting NASCAR pit procedures, some plants managed to reduce downtime to as little as 20 minutes.

World Traveler Magazine, March 2002

Just because you have not exercised your imagination lately does not mean that you have lost this wonderful capability. It's waiting to be unleashed. Remind yourself and trust that creativity is in fact the true nature you were born with.

N stands for NOMINAL STRESS (CREATIVE TENSION)

For the violin string to produce the right tone it needs the right amount of stress. Under too much tension the string snaps and with no tension it does not produce any music.

Similarly the mind needs creative tension. Creative tension is the gap between where we are and where we want to be.

How many times have you come out of the shower with a solution to a problem that had been on your mind? You had a good night's sleep and were relaxed in general. In this state the neurons were playing around and making new connections to resolve the tension. To make new connections the mind needs to be in a playful mode.

An overly stressed mind is not in a creative mode. When under stress the neurons take the path of least resistance – the known pathways. When facing change the response then becomes, "This is the way we've always done things around here." An overly stressed mind says, "Don't talk to me about the future. Let me get through today."

George Ballas was experiencing creative tension from trying to mow his tree-packed lawn. To solve this problem he created a prototype Weed Eater from a tin can and fishing wire.

The role of leaders is to set specific goals for improving business processes, cost structure, customer experience, and so on, the goal being a stretch, that is, far enough to require greater effort but not too far away to be unattainable. This creates the required creative tension and gets the creative problem-solving journey started.

Example: You're in a meeting and the boss at the beginning of the meeting gives a general talk about the competitive environment or the global economy and states that he wants everyone to think creatively and be innovative. Everyone sitting around the table is feeling stressed and wondering, "What does he mean, 'be creative and innovative'?" This reaction occurs because there is no specific improvement target for the activity/function that you can do something about.

Netflix, the movie rental company, set a goal of improving the movie recommendations made by its internal software by at least 10 percent, as measured by predicted-versus-actual one-through-five star ratings provided by customers, and offered a $1 million prize to the winner. This provided the creative tension to engage creative minds all over the world in addressing this challenge.

T stands for TIME

Creative problem solving requires time to engage the mind in exploring "what if" before locking into "how to." Also, it takes time to develop a raw creative idea and get it ready for implementation.

If you're constantly running from one meeting to another, where is the time to think? Your busy calendar must reflect a balance between doing and thinking by scheduling some quiet time to just think. For example, Intuit, an accounting and financial software provider, gives its employees 10% of their hours as unstructured time, time to think creatively for improving Intuit products and services.

Another well-proven avenue is taking time to ask "why" – to question current assumptions. Hertz, Avis, and other large companies assumed that people rent cars when they travel. The Enterprise rental car company team questioned that assumption by observing that people also need cars when their vehicle is being repaired. They also often need cars when having normal maintenance done at the dealership. Enterprise set up a system to deliver cars to customers at home, dealers, or repair shops. This allowed them to develop a very successful business in an untapped market segment.

So, to recap:

- Gathering raw material, expanding your knowledge base, takes time.

- Processing the raw material into new products (that is, making new connections) requires time.

- All creative ideas when first generated are raw. They need to be developed to get them ready for implementation. This last important step in the three-step innovation process also needs time.

How balance helps in creating more dots: The first condition

Dr. Phil, a popular TV host, regularly advises the guests on his show, "You can't take care of others until you take care of yourself – you need balance and joy in your life. Think back to a time before you became consumed by your job. What were your passions then? Did you enjoy jogging? Painting? Travel? Identify what excites and relaxes you, then make time to do it."

A balanced lifestyle with time allocated for hobbies and new experiences helps create more dots, the first condition for making new connections. You're not short changing your career when taking time to pursue relaxing hobbies.

Human beings have habits which can be self-satisfying and self-fulfilling. An integral part of that habit is development of hobbies. In the life of the average man, his wife and children, his work and financial position occupy the main part of his anxious and serious thought. Hobbies provide leisure and afford relaxation from the tenseness of his more serious pre-occupations. A major source of unhappiness, fatigue and nervousness is the inability to be interested in anything that's not of practical importance in one's life.

Varkha Chulani, Clinical Psychologist, Lilavati Hospital, March 9, 2008, Times Wellness,

Vacations, with their extended time for play, rest, and relaxation, provide some degree of distance to take in the big picture. We get an opportunity to reflect on what really matters. The daily round is so assertive in its demands that we do not have the privilege of considering the wider perspective of what we are really going to do with the years ahead of us. We know what we want to be--a top rate marketing manager, engineer, accountant--but it does not answer the question how we really want to spend our life.

Every now and then go away,
have a little relaxation
for when you come back
to your work
your judgment will be surer;
since to remain constantly at work
will cause you to lose power
of judgment

Go some distance away
because the work appears smaller
and more of it
can be taken in at a glance,
and a lack of harmony
or proportion
is more readily seen

Leonardo Da Vinci (1452-1519)

Reading, attending lectures, taking Classes just for the fun of it ... Be a learner

Our minds can only think to the breadth they are exposed to. So expose yourself to as many fields as possible.

The creative person wants to be know-it-all. He wants to know about all kinds of things: ancient history, nineteenth-century mathematics, current manufacturing techniques, flower arranging, and hog futures. Because he never knows when these ideas might

145

come together to form a new idea. It may happen six minutes later or six months down the road. But he has faith that it will happen.

CARL ALLY, whose agency was responsible for the creative and memorable ads that helped FedEx become a household name

Living things in nature want to grow.

Just like the plants and trees, growth is a basic human need. For an apple tree, the growth is sprouting a new branch. The branch becomes strong, sprouting a flower and then an apple — all manifestations of growth.

Similarly, a child experiences growth when she or he takes the first steps or learns to say "mama" and "dada." As adults, we experience growth in the Career Self when we learn new skills or solve a challenging problem. We experience growth in the People Self by making new friends or by making existing relationships deeper. We experience growth in the actualizing self when we grow spiritually. We experience growth in the Leisure Self, for example, when we finally master that overhead shot in tennis.

The growth need is met when a person does something or experiences something that is new to him or her. It does not matter to an apple tree that there are millions of other apple trees that have produced apples. It is growth for the apple tree that it has grown and is producing apples.

To live and grow requires an ecologically balanced environment.

The plants need a healthy balance of sunlight, water and nutrition from the soil. Too much water and not enough sunlight disturb the balance and retard the plant growth. The simple act of moving the houseplant closer to a window restores the balance and the growth.

A stable, mature and happy family life may well allow one more time and energy to devote to the workplace than does a family life fraught with problems. Putting it differently, avoiding a bad family life may really pay off.

A study by Cappelli of Wharton School, Jill Constantine of Williams College and Clint Chadwick of Wharton, contradicts other studies as well as the conventional wisdom that those who put family over career will earn lower wages.

> Our growth as a human being is stifled when our lifestyle becomes unbalanced. The vitality, the inner energy stops renewing itself, and we feel restless and tired.

When the ecological balance is disturbed, the plants and marine life begin to die.

We've all read of how once-healthy lakes became polluted and the marine life disappeared. Or how, in some rivers or lakes where the marine life is not completely dead, the growth has been retarded, and the size of the fish is much smaller than before. Similarly, our growth as a human being is stifled when our lifestyle becomes unbalanced. The vitality, the inner energy stops renewing itself, and we feel restless and tired. We go through the motions and may even have many external trappings of success, but feel unfulfilled as human beings.

There is more to life than increasing its speed. –Mahatma Gandhi

When we slow down, quiet the mind, and allow ourselves to feel hungry for something that we do not understand, we are dipping into the abundant well of spiritual longing.

- Elizabeth Lesser, from her book The Seeker's Guide: Making Your Life a Spiritual Adventure

How balanced life helps develop imagination: The second condition

Your imagination is a right brain capability. To unleash that part of your brain, find ways to:

- Actively pursue interests and hobbies.

    There is a part of me that wants to write, a part that wants to sculpt, a part that wants to teach ... To force myself into a single role, to decide to be just one thing in life, would kill off large part of me.

    Hugh Prather, Notes to Myself

- Participate in and observe artistic endeavors – music, art, theater.

- Spend time in nature.

Writing books is both a left and right brain activity. My engineering education in India and the U.S. was entirely focused on developing and using analytical/left brain capabilities. Spending time in nature – hiking in the woods, climbing mountains, boating on the river, relaxing on the beach, and snorkeling in the ocean has been very helpful in developing my imagination/right brain capabilities.

- Play with children.

    I get my innovation inspiration from children. They have an amazing ability to change ordinary objects into whatever they need them to be by using their imagination. They have the ability to see beyond what is in front of them and create new uses for items. I marvel at how my children can turn a bedroom into a sea. The bed into a pirate ship, pillows into sharks and empty paper towel roles into swords.

    JAMIE WOOLF,
    Learning and Development Specialist, Kimberly-Clark

As difficult as it may be for some people to believe, relaxing is NOT a waste of time. Without proper rest, both your body and mind become exhausted and your creative juices dry up. Adequate sleep, relaxation and fun are must for avoiding burnout.

Apple co-founder Steve Jobs practiced Zen Buddhist meditation techniques daily. "If you just sit and observe, you will see how restless your mind is," Jobs told his biographer Walter Isaacson. "If you try to calm it, it only makes things worse, but over time it does calm, and when it does, there's room to hear more subtle things — that's when your intuition starts to blossom and you start to see things more clearly and be in the present. Your mind just slows down, and you see a tremendous expanse in the moment. You see so much than you could see before. It's a discipline; you have to practice it."

A balanced life celebrating life in its fullness does not put all eggs in the career basket. The multiple sources of joy are the foundation for feeling secure, prerequisite for setting and achieving innovation goals.

How balanced life provides inner security to take risk in setting 'Innovation goals/creative tension (Nominal stress)': The third condition

Someone who gets all of his kicks from work cannot afford to take any risk. Creativity means taking the risk in challenging the status quo.

A violin cannot play a sweet note unless the strings are under pressure. But if you put too much pressure on the strings, they snap. So do we. When the violin is not being used, you release the tension on the strings. We too need periods of relaxation to recover and renew.

- Tanya Wheway

As we discussed earlier balanced life needs are not optional. The unmet needs do not go away they create conflicts and stress. Setting and taking steps to meet PAL goals is the only path to reducing inner tension, caused by expecting the job to fulfill emotional and spiritual needs.

The greater the congruence between inner wishes and conscious goals, the greater the available energy. To use my teacher's image, you must have both the bubbling up of thoughts and the capacity to release them. We all have, in varying degrees, this constant generation of images and ideas. The trick is to capture and harness them to make them work for us. Too much 'viscosity'--fear and unresolved feelings that oppose the effective expression of these ideas--can get in the way."

Anna Fels, M.D

How Balance helps create Time to think: The fourth condition

At lunch I will go out and bike 20 miles. Then I'll get back and all of a sudden a thought comes to my brain, and I solve something I was struggling with. Goodnight (CEO of SAS) understands the innovative process, and there's time built for it.

Mary Simmons, principle software developer, SAS, FORTUNE, August 17, 2009

Edison's friends in Florida respected his need for privacy. He would go out to the end of his dock and sit and fish – but he'd fish without any bait on his line. Edison was not interested in catching fish; he was after time to think.

James Newton, Uncommon Friends, Harcourt Brace, 1987

Almost all innovations, whether technical, political, or social come from thinking deeply about the subject. That means taking time to learn, think, and imagine. My most favorite mini-vacations are long weekends on a lake or in the mountains. Recently we rented a cabin on Lake Ouachita in Arkansas, a beautiful hideaway with woods surrounding the lake. In addition to being very relaxing, the hours spent on the cabin deck with the smart phone turned off, were very productive in generating ideas for this book.

When I travel long distances, I fly business class to get peace and quiet. I try not to drink alcohol or watch TV. Instead I take the time to think. A lot of my ideas come from that quiet time.

Sam Jain, founder, Fareportal and CheapOair
Fortune, December 1, 2114

Taking mandatory day off every week has done wonders for my productivity. I realized a few years back that I used to burn out every few months, and it was happening increasingly. By taking one full day off, I was able to give my body and brain a much needed break that allowed me to come back to work refreshed.

Apoorva Mehta, Instacart founder
Fortune, October 1, 2015

Becoming an Innovation Leader

Whereas creativity deals solely with the generation of ideas by exploring "what if" scenarios, innovation starts with creative ideas but takes the process two steps further.

Innovation does not just happen. It must be actively supported. Individual employee creativity is the first step of innovation. Managers/team leaders have to create an environment where employees feel comfortable in suggesting and experimenting with new ways of doing things.

An innovation culture actively promotes the three stages of innovation:

- Generation
- Acceptance
- Implementation

It's people who have creative ideas. It's people who accept and develop the raw creative ideas. It's people who successfully implement the developed ideas. Leaders at all levels of the organization play the single most important role in creating and sustaining the supportive environment that actively engages people in the innovation process, developing and unleashing employees' natural creative potential at all levels of the organization.

In fact, about 75 percent of ideas that result in better products or services for companies come from front-line workers. When management finds ways to harness that creativity, firms reap benefits.

**ALAN ROBINSON, Corporate Creativity:
How Innovation and Improvement Actually Happen**

How unresolved life balance conflicts impact leadership effectiveness

Leader needs to actively solicit and listen to employees' creative ideas. If the leader is insecure, he will not take the risks involved in exploring new ways. Controlled by the unchecked ego, the leader thinks he has the right answer, directed by this message, the mind stops looking for new information. The person stops listening and stifles creativity in the organization. A balanced life helps keep the ego in check.

Successful leadership presupposes having much of one's own psychological house in order. It becomes a tough balancing act. These conflicts have to be dealt with because if they're ignored, they don't just go away. Suppressed feelings develop into compensating behaviors that are not conducive to effective innovation leadership.

A Balanced Lifestyle with time for exercise keeps mind sharp

A morning workout triggers feel-good endorphins and lowers elevated stress hormones. The effects can last six to eight hours, says Gregory Florez, a spokesperson for the American Council on Exercise, in Salt Lake City. "Morning exercisers tend not to have midmorning slumps and are sharper mentally than if they hadn't exercised." You'll get the most bangs for your energy buck, he says, with a workout that includes both cardio and strength training.

Time to Wake Up!
Real Simple magazine, May 2011

A balanced lifestyle with control on internet time frees time for what matters

I actually have been thinking a lot about this. I work full time and have a 1.5 year old. I often feel that I've wasted away my day, but it is because I spend so much time on the internet. When I finally put away my phone and do something (cook, exercise, spend time with my husband, my hobbies!) I feel so much better. Check email here, facebook and twitter there and soon we've been online for hours each day. I truly think that phones and the internet are sucking what we used to know as life away from us. Just like keeping a food diary often illuminates what we really are eating, keeping a time diary would show how much time we spend online.

Anne from Chicago commenting on
LAURA VANDERKAM's article
'The Busy Person's Lies' in The New York Times,
May 13, 2016

Studies have shown conclusively that every time we interrupt what we're doing to check email, messages, Facebook posts, or the latest Twitter feed, it takes at least 15 minutes for the mind to get back to where it was before the interruption. The mind needs at least 15 concentration-filled minutes to get into the zone where it can think deeply and make new connections, i.e. think creatively.

Chapter 9

Enterprise Growth, Creativity and Balance: The Three Legged Stool

---

For sustained growth in today's fast changing and highly competitive global economy, companies need both – an innovative growth strategy, and flawless execution of that strategy. **Innovative Growth Strategy + Flawless Execution = Enterprise Growth.**

'Our people are our most important assets.' This statement has been voiced by companies' senior management and written in CEOs' letters accompanying the annual reports for years. It holds truer today than ever before, because it is the people who develop a company's innovative growth strategy and it is the people who flawlessly execute that strategy to deliver a competitively superior value day in and day out.

My firsthand experience as a member of the management team responsible for FedEx's global growth, is that creative thinking and innovation aren't only required while developing strategies. They gain much more importance in the development of detailed execution plans. For successful execution, the enterprise strategy has to be translated into innovative and functional strategies for all moving parts of the organization – Operations, Marketing, Sales, Human Resources, Logistics,

IT, etc. This requires the application of creative thinking to all functional areas.

People don't come to work in the morning, flip a switch and say, "now that I'm at work, I'll forget everything else going in my life." They come to work as whole individuals with lives and needs that extend beyond work. Unfulfilled life needs, whether on-the-job or off-the-job, do not simply go away. They create conflicts within and without the individual. Conflicts lead to stress, and a stressed mind is not in a creative mode. A stressed mind is in a survival mode.

> Happiness and creativity are the natural by-products of a balanced lifestyle, celebrating life in its fullness.

A former jazz pianist and physicist at the Fermi National Accelerator Laboratory, Blakely was one of the principal architects of Microsoft's Xbox. When creative people are happy, they do better work.

Jamin Brophy-Warren,
Fast Company, April 2010

Happiness makes people more productive at work, according to the latest research from the University of Warwick. They found happiness made people 12% more productive. The driving force seems to be that happier workers use the time they have more effectively, increasing the pace at which they can work without sacrificing quality.

Andrew J Oswald and Eugenio Proto,
University of Warwick

Visualize enterprise growth, creativity and balance as the legs of a three legged stool. For the stool to continue to fulfill its function and remain stable and strong, all of its three legs must be equally strong. Each leg of the stool has an equally important role in supporting the other two legs. Similarly, an enterprise is nothing but a group of people working collaboratively and supporting each other to achieve a common goal. Every employee plays an important role, indispensable like a leg of the stool. .

As part of my engineering studies at BITS Pilani, I did a summer internship at Hindustan Motors. At that time, the Ambassador car manufactured by Hindustan Motors was in big demand and considered an undisputed market leader. In fact, people had to wait for months to get their orders fulfilled. The company was the largest car manufacturer in India.

After enjoying a market leading position for a long period, Hindustan Motors started losing market share, and finally in 2014 it stopped manufacturing the Ambassador. Similarly, once global market leaders in their respective industries, Kodak, Xerox and Blackberry ended up losing a significant market shares along with their coveted leadership status.

How did that happen?

No company exists in a vacuum. It exists in a larger business environment comprised of customers, competitors - local and global, government regulations, technology and other factors. If there is no change in the larger business environment then companies can keep doing the business the way they've been doing and safely maintain their market share. But to grow in a changing business environment, a company's internal rate of change (new business strategy, business processes, products, distribution systems etc.

> To grow in a changing business environment, a company's internal rate of change must be greater than the external rate of change.

controlled by the company) must be greater than the external rate of change (changes outside the control of the company). If the external rate of change exceeds the internal rate of change, the company will lose its competitive edge and market share.

The arrows 1 and 2 in the figure 9.1 below represent the squeeze put on companies by the rate of change in the larger business environment (external changes) where competition occurs. The only way to neutralize this external pressure and gain market share is to counter it with a higher internal rate of change, arrow 3.

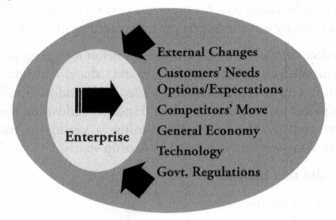

The first step in gaining market share is having an understanding of the changes taking place in the larger business environment. The second step is engaging the enterprise in developing innovative solutions to capitalize on the opportunities presented by the changes. In today's fast changing business environment the speed in developing and implementing innovative solutions is the key to staying ahead of the competition and increasing market share.

Is the rate of change going to slow down?

Absolutely not!

Therefore, the only sustainable competitive edge in today's fast changing global economy is continuous innovation.

Who is responsible for change and innovation in the organization?

Everyone. It is leaders' responsibility to engage employees in the innovation process of generation, acceptance and implementation of creative ideas to stay ahead of the competition. Successful implementation of creative ideas requires commitment at all levels.

Why leaders don't encourage and expect innovation as a matter of course?

Too often they are internally focused – fully occupied with what's happening inside the organization. There is no process or expectation to keep up with the changes in the larger business environment they compete in - the external world.

Leaders' behavior plays a key role in tapping into employees' creativity and commitment

There is enormous untapped potential found in the employees of most large organizations. The manager's behavior plays a key role in tapping this discretionary effort.

> The ability to tap creativity and the latent commitment of everyone in an organization is demonstrably the one unifying theme found in the achievements of all great organizations.

When working with organizations to build an innovation culture, I start the process by placing select employees and managers into four small groups and asking each group to answer one of the following four questions:

Group 1: Why should you worry about innovation?

Group 2: What would innovation look like in your areas of responsibility?

Group 3: How do you create an environment that promotes innovative thinking at all levels of the organization?

Group 4: What stops you from developing and unleashing your creative potential?

The responses to question number four almost typically reveal that leadership practices have prevented employees from engaging in innovative thinking and creative problem solving. These innovation-squashing leadership practices and organizational support systems include:

- Discouraging change
- Not being open to looking at different ways of doing things
- Micromanaging
- Resisting challenges by employees
- Bureaucratic systems that slow things down
- Indecisive management
- Lack of time for creative thinking due to busy schedules
- Turf protections as a result of departmental isolation and lack of collaboration or cross-pollination between departments
- Lack of challenging goals and direction
- Inability of managers to discuss conflicting ideas on a professional level
- Close-minded managers who are not willing to listen to new ideas
- A culture that suggests that in order to get ahead one must not make waves and must play politically safe
- Fear of failure

It's been my experience that the majority of managers do possess the capacity to articulate the desirable leadership behaviors that will inspire employees to develop and unleash their creative potential. So why is there such a large gap between intellectual understanding of the right leadership behaviors/practices and their application on the job? There are several reasons. The first is a lack of real understanding that three equally important skill sets – technical, managerial, and leadership – are all required for successful outcomes.

Secondly, there is a lack of awareness that effective leadership is the result of a completely distinct skill set, more of an affair of the heart (right-brain) than the head (left-brain). Psychological research has shown that the left side of the brain is the place for segmented, analytical and rational processes. The right side supports conceptual, creative and feeling processes. The analytical side makes for good planners, organizers and controllers – and thus, effective managers. The feeling and conceptual side makes for visionary, caring and inspiring managers – and thus effective leaders.

> Effective leadership is the result of a completely distinct skill set, more of an affair of the heart (right-brain) than the head (left-brain).

Supported by authority, rules and regulations, you can get people to work at 60 to 65 percent capacity — just enough to satisfy minimum job requirements. Leadership is a multiplier factor that deals with the other 35 to 40 percent. A mere administrator can achieve average results. The leader gets superior results from average people. Management is largely an action-oriented cerebral process. Leadership is principally an action-oriented inter-personal process.

— James J. Cribbin, AMA, New York
Leadership: Strategies for Organizational Efficiency

Drivers of Leadership (Human) Behaviors

"Why is he behaving this way?" It's a familiar question. To understand the visible behavior we need to understand some of the invisible factors operating in the background. What the person knows, how he feels and how supportive the environment is, play a major role in answering the question. A person may know how to do the job, but if he feels disengaged, he is not going to go out of his way to take initiative in identifying and solving problems. A person may have an innovative idea, but if risk is not encouraged, success is not rewarded and failure is punished, he is not going to take the risk. Harry Levinson summed up the central role feelings play at work and how difficult it is for so many managers to deal with them in his review of Manfred F. R. Kets de Vries' book, Life and Death in the Executive Fast Lane.

'Is management in reality a rational task performed by rational people according to sensible organizational objectives?' We all know better, yet the myth of rationality persists in spite of all evidence to the contrary. Much of our society and most of our business life is organized around airtight logic, numbers, and explanations that 'make sense.' However, a whole range of logic-defying emotions – rage, fear, insecurity, jealousy, and passion – is acted out in the office. It is these powerful yet unacknowledged feelings that often disrupt our organization.

"Most executives have a notoriously underdeveloped capacity for understanding and dealing with emotions. All but the best are reluctant to ask the selves why they act the way they do. As a result, most fail to understand both their own managerial behavior and that of others."

Harry Levinson in January/February 1996 Harvard Business Review, review of the book, "Life and Death in the Executive Fast Lane" by Manfred F.R. Kets de Vries

Even when we have a fairly optimum balanced life, and we function wellon the job at one stage of our life, we must realize that as we grow and change in our job while also growing chronologically older, our personal needs change as well. Such change can be extraordinarily disruptive and — unless understood as a natural part of human development — potentially destructive.

Many times, we are not prepared for how these unperceived changes affect our commitments to particular relationships, career goals, and chosen lifestyles. Such change most certainly creates tension between our various selves (CPAL) and with others. As we assume more responsibilities at work or in our personal lives, our needs and goals compete for the limited personal resources of time and energy, and conflict with each other as well as with the reality of the outside world. Psychological studies have shown the primary source of the dilemmas that leaders face is their own inner conflicts.

Leadership Effectiveness and Balance

During my 2015 India visit I facilitated several 'Balanced Life' sessions for managers in Mumbai and Pune. One of the questions answered by the groups was:

What is the impact of an unbalanced life on your professional/leadership effectiveness?

They answered.

- Stress leading to lack of concentration

- Lack of efficiency

- Disturbed mind/impatient with people we are leading

- Getting worked-up/panic

- Not able to think creatively

To lead successfully presupposes having much of one's own psychological house in order. It becomes a tough balancing act. These unpleasant feelings have to be dealt with, because if ignored, they don't just go away. Suppressed feelings develop into compensating behaviors that are not conducive to effective leadership.

> We're most creative and open to receiving the flow of creative ideas from self and others when we're at peace.

Leading for Innovation: Tapping Employees' Creativity and Commitment

Leadership Behavior to Tap Employees' Creativity	Compensating Behavior Created by Unresolved Work/Life Balance Conflicts
To meet employees' need for feeling that the corporate culture and leaders expect and support change (create MINT conditions) 1. Change your paradigm from viewing employees as a set of hands to viewing them as a source of ideas. Allow time to think and listen.	1. People who are preoccupied with themselves pay only superficial attention to other people. They are so tied up in themselves that they cannot observe the subtleties in another person's feelings, nor can they really listen. As a result, they cannot really respond to other people as individuals.
2. Help employees enhance their self-esteem by creating an environment that encourages people to experiment and take risks.	2. Because of a manager's low frustration tolerance, subordinates are afraid to voice their opinions. Relationships based on fear are not healthy or conducive to spontaneity and enhancing self-esteem.

3. Expect employees to innovate by regularly asking them what specific changes they have made lately.	3. If a manager is insecure and fears failure, he will not take the risk involved in starting new project sand exploring new ways of doing things. She or he will block the organization's creative potential for developing and implementing innovative solutions.

Tapping Employees' Commitment

A committed (mind) employee can be expected to

- Go an extra mile to satisfy the customer with an attitude of 'whatever it takes.'

- Work independently, without supervision

- Make sound decisions on the organization's behalf even in an unfamiliar situation

- Go beyond formal job descriptions

To tap into employees' commitment the leader must connect with and inspire them. Being analytical all the time makes us inaccessible. People connect to people at the feeling level.

Before we can connect with others, we have to connect to our selves, that is, have access to our feeling/human self. When we lead a balanced life to connect with and meet the needs of our PAL (human self), we're unleashing our leadership potential.

It's Unhappiness, Not the Workload

Bangalore techies are known to suffer from psychological disorders. But if you thought it's just work pressure, think again.

Around 93 percent of corporate Bangalore is unhappy at work, reports a health risk assessment study conducted by People Health, a health management organization, on 2,106 employees of seven leading IT firms in the city. Unhappiness among employees was primarily due to a combination of long office hours, hostile work atmosphere, uncooperative colleagues and rude bosses. These seem to create more negative feelings than not getting a promotion or pay hike, reports the study.

Damayanti Datta,
November 23, 2009, India Today

Leadership Behavior to Tap Employees' Commitment	Compensating Behavior Created by Unresolved Work/Life Balance Conflicts
To meet employees' need for feeling part of a team that is going places, 1. Translate corporate vision for department and share with the group. Vision is a mental picture not of what we are, but of what we need to be. How are we going to get from here to there? Shared vision molds individuals into a common direction. The leader almost has to be evangelical about it.	1. "Busy Executive" driven by the need to control is so tied up in the day-to-day details that he or she does not have time for stepping back and conceptualizing the bigger picture — developing a vision. Before a manager can expect his vision to be shared by subordinates, he needs to have a vision.
2. To meet employees' need for wanting a say in how we go about doing our jobs, Involve others by actively soliciting solutions to problems.	2. Unresolved career and personal concerns create inner tension, which interferes with a person's ability to integrate and use information — the most important step in problem solving and decision making.
3. Be sensitive to the fact that employees' have a life beyond work.	3. It's very hard to be sensitive to other's balance needs if he is not sensitive to his own.

If you're successful at making your company a happy place, every day is awesome.

Caterina Flake, Founder and CEO, Findery, and Chairman of the board, Etsy

How organizations can help their most important asset, people, stay in peak performing state

For too many years, we have treated employee development, work satisfaction and job motivation as if they existed apart from the fullness and richness of an employee's life. The reality is that employees do not live neat, compartmentalized lives in which each separate concern operates within a closed system.

In fact, off-the-job concerns affect the employee on the job and viceversa. An employee's psychological well-being and his or her work effectiveness go hand-in-hand.

The success of a business depends on the people within the organization. If the heart, the passion and the focus of a person is not involved in his or her job, the organization suffers.

The competitive edge rests with the companies who retain the best management resources to achieve their corporate goals. The new breed of professionals and managers are different than their predecessors. The economic manager is being superseded by the psychological manager — managers for whom what Maslow called "the higher needs" have become important.

With the material needs satisfied, the need for challenging and significant work, for fulfilling relationships, and for a stimulating and fulfilling life experience become the prime motivating factor. When these needs are not met, frustration sets in.

It is abundantly clear that personal off-the-job concerns do affect the manager on the job. Therefore, neither the corporation nor the manager can continue to look at work and career in isolation from other aspects of the manager's life. Because the growth and productivity of organizations is more than ever dependent on the effectiveness of human performance, the corporations who choose to ignore this vital issue do so at a great cost to themselves. When the people in the organization grow, the organization grows. It is in the organization's self-interest to help employees lead a balanced lifestyle.

Finally, in the 21st Century, the Return on Investment — the bottom line measurement — will be directly related to:

- Return on Ideas and Innovation,
- Return on Initiative
- Return on Interpersonal Relationships

The Ideas, Initiative and Interpersonal returns from leadership are by products of a work force that is able to access all of its inner resources.

Integrate, 'Leading for Innovation and Balance: A Nurturing Relationship' in leadership development.

At Lilly, we survive and thrive in the business of discovering and developing innovative pharmaceutical products. To do this, we depend on our employees' brainpower and creativity, their initiative and their alignment with our goals for the business, and we need these at every level in the business...

Organizations that cannot respond to their employees as total human beings will stagnate and become less efficient than those organizations better able to assist their managers in successfully achieving both their career and personal balanced-life goals.

A company can't hire just part of a person – you get the sore back along with skillful hands, you get the anxious heart along with educated and creative brain. So our policies and our programs will be effective only if we address this reality and if we acknowledge our employees for what they are – whole people. We should not just allow but encourage them to have lives beyond work.

Randall Tobias, CEO,
Eli Lilly and Company

It would be ideal if all humans were taught two basics equally: 1) how to make a living and 2) how to live a balanced life that reflects one's values and priorities. One learns the basics about a chosen profession through school and college work. Then one gets practical hands-on training in the business world. But no one teaches how to live a balanced life. That's something a person often has to seek out for himself.

I asked a very successful friend at our twenty-fifth alumni reunion of the Harvard Business School for his measure of success. He said, "I learned to smell the roses."

Robert Medearis, Chairman,
Silicon Valley Bank

Leadership is an extension of who one is: the whole person, the analytical side and the feeling side – the whole human. Anything that affects a person, also affects his or her leadership abilities. Certainly it is a balancing act that requires one to think in a way that at first is unfamiliar and not what most are used to, but the payoff is huge and long-lasting.

Leaders are paid for the quality and creativity of their decisions and the decisions made by their staffs, not for the hours worked. When leaders take time for personal lives, it helps to develop and unleash his or her feeling and imaginative side, the creative side. People need to give themselves permission to celebrate life in its fullness.

Interpersonal skills (how we deal with others) are directly related to intra-personal skills (how we deal with ourselves). It is very difficult to be sensitive to work/life balance needs of others if one is not sensitive to his own balance needs.

Where a person is in life is a cumulative result of all the choices, big and small, a person has made so far. To improve the quality of life and balance in life, one must improve how one makes choices.

I was speaking with the vice president of Human Resources of a Fortune 500 company that offers a wide range of work/life benefits. The Human Resources department had just completed an organization-wide survey regarding the company's benefit programs. One of the key findings of the survey was that employees really appreciated the various work/life benefits made available by the company, but employees were not comfortable using them because their immediate supervisors did not support or encourage their use. That's the result of a lack of awareness of the direct relationship between employees' work performance and life balance.

The managers had not internalized the fact that once a person becomes a manager, his performance is measured by how well his employees do and the employee performance reflects the quality of management. The following unwritten employment contract with the new breed of workers illustrates this relationship.

In order to be the most effective leader, one must dare to be the most complete human being he or she can be. A person becomes complete and whole by celebrating life in its fullness, by leading a balanced life.

Level I contribution: I need a job to pay for my basic needs (fulfilling the needs of the body). You give me a job, and

I will give you just enough to keep my job.

Level II contribution: If the job is interesting and challenging (fulfilling the needs of the mind in addition to meeting the basic needs), then I will give to the job much more than the minimum daily requirement.

Level III contribution: If the job, the organization, and the manager makes me feel valued as a person with a life outside the job and provides a sense of meaning and contribution to the community at-large (fulfilling the needs of the spirit, mind and body), then I will give you all I have to offer – creativity and commitment.

During my tenure at the FedEx Leadership Institute I was the team leader for a week long leadership development course for newly promoted managing directors. I worked with Thonda Barnes, the course designer and one of the most innovative persons I've ever had the pleasure to work with in the corporate world. Together we presented the course 'Leading for Innovation & Balance: A Nurturing Relationship.'

The learning objectives for this module were:

1. Understand the mutually supportive relationships between professional and personal effectiveness, that is, leadership excellence and work/life balance.

2. Understand how your ability to model and support work/life balance creates a caring environment and enhances your leadership ability to tap discretionary effort – FedEx's competitive edge.

3. Develop a personalized action plan addressing the root causes, internal and external, of imbalance in your unique environment.

4. Understand the role of leadership and work/life balance in unleashing the organization's innovation capacity.

Senior Management Leading By Example

When Shelly Lazarus, head of Ogilvy & Mather Worldwide, tells her employees to get a life outside the office, she means it. That's because she sees outside interests and commitments as a sine qua non of O&M's chief asset: Creativity. Lazarus once skipped a board meeting in Paris to go on a ski trip with her family. "People were horrified ... (but) you must keep your perspective, it's only business."

Global Literacies by Robert Rosen
Anne Fisher, Best Business Books, May 15, 2000, Fortune

When you realize, as I did that lack of balance downgrades your effectiveness, it's easy to make balancea priority. I finally understand that achieving balance would actually help my career. I work to have a good quality of life, not to achieve some arbitrary goal, such as job title or a figure in a bank account.

David Lunsford, Director of Advanced Technology, Dell Computer Corporation

'Balance,' a key factor in recruiting, retaining and engaging the best and the brightest

Several years ago, I spoke at international conferences organized by the Society of Human Resources and Management (SHRM) in Monterey, California and New York. The topic of my talk at both conferences was the 'Key Role of Balance in Attracting and Retaining the Best and the Brightest.'

The Monterey session was attended by over 100 senior Human Resource (HR) managers. After the talk, several attendees approached me to share a common sentiment - "We hear constantly from our employees about their work/life balance needs, but when I go to my president, he says, 'That's nice but we've got a business to run.' Can you meet with my president?" I had one free day before my return flight to Memphis, so I agreed to stop by at two companies the following day.

I had good conversations with the presidents at both companies. They understood the criticality of innovation in staying ahead of the competition, but I sensed the enormous pressure that both presidents were under in trying to meet the next quarter's financial targets. I shared with them my research on the mutually supportive relationship between 'Balance' and 'Creativity,' and suggested changing the business script from quantity of hours to quality and creativity in work.

As per an online poll conducted by market research firm AC Nielsen, 74% of Indian respondents said they preferred to be in a work that was not the all-consuming thing in their lives. A whopping 82% in their 20s said attaining a work-life balance was priority in the New Year.

However, AC Nielsen pointed out that Indians were not unique in clamoring for more personal time in the coming year. Exercise and better work/life balance also took the top two places for people making resolutions in other parts of the world.

The Times of India Online

Findings of a global study, conducted by Mercer and reported in USA Today, showed, 'most workers say that being treated with respect is most important, followed by work/life balance, type of work, quality of co-workers and quality of leadership.' Organizations that don't understand the importance of these hard-to-quantify benefits risk losing the employees they've invested in. The turnovers can be very expensive.

In employees' minds and in some managers' minds, work and life are closely linked to Baxter's Shared Value of Respect. Without respecting an employee's life outside the workplace, there cannot be true respect for the individual. For managers and employees who are supportive of work and life, a key reason why is because they believe, as the CFO stated, "Work and life are a critical element of how we treat people."

Alice Campbell, Director Work/Life Initiatives
Baxter Healthcare Corporation

While speaking to Wipro employees in Hyderabad, the subject of work/life balance came up. I shared with the group that since my wife works full time, we both share duties at home, e.g., she loads the dish washer, I empty it; she does the laundry, I fold it; when both kids have after school activities, we split our driving duties. If I get home before her, I warm up the food and keep it ready.

Women in the Wipro team started laughing and shared that their husbands don't do any of this. Women, who work, have two full-time jobs, one outside and one at home. Initiatives to build an environment supportive of work/life balance become even more important for attracting and retaining women employees.

Women who are ambitious and passionate about their careers have to make many sacrifices as from the time of marriage to childbirth and much later they hardly find relief from responsibilities like childcare and home management ('Business Bottomline' page – "'Daughterly guilt' haunts Indian working women, March 21.) This is because in a country like India – and despite making noises about gender equality – men are not trained in household duties and a woman is forced to do almost everything. The erosion of the joint family system has also destroyed supportive facilities for a woman. If employers really care about retaining efficient women staff even after childbirth they should enable the provision of day-care centers on their premises, 'flexi-time' opportunities and 'work from home' facilities.

Rameeza A. Rasheed, Letter to Editor,
March 23, 2016, The Hindu, Chennai

Flexible Work Arrangements

Flextime – Employees work a regular schedule, but start and end their day (e.g., earlier or later) around business and personal needs.

Part Time – Employees work 20 - 30 hours per week with regularly scheduled hours, eligible for the same benefits as full-time employees, but on an adjusted basis.

Job Sharing – Two employees split the hours, workload and pay of one full time job.

Compressed Work Week – A full time schedule that is considered into fewer and longer days (e.g., four 10-hour days)

Telecommuting – Employees work from home on a regular or occasional basis. If working from home is not feasible then company can look into establishing satellite offices around the city to reduce commute time. In large cities because of traffic congestion and lack of affordable housing close to work, commuting to work can take 1-2 hours.

Reducing healthcare costs and keeping employees healthy

- To control healthcare costs, businesses are initiating Wellness/Well-being Programs

- Businesses and insurance companies are offering wellness tests, financial incentives, newsletters and information on their websites

When practiced on a sustained basis, wellness programs have proven to be very effective in controlling healthcare costs. Currently however, only a small percentage of employees are enrolling in and staying with the wellness programs. The challenge is to engage a majority of employees for maximizing the benefits (healthcare cost reduction).

The primary reason for this gap between the desired goal and reality:

- The ultimate responsibility for the success of Wellness initiatives lies with each individual employee

- If an employee feels that by taking time out for Wellness, they may be shortchanging their career and hurting their chances for the next promotion, then they won't be motivated to get involved and stay with a program

- **"I don't really have time for personal/family life or to exercise/go to the gym."**

Stress is a fact of life that we can neither avoid nor eliminate. A wellness oriented, balanced lifestyle has time and activities built-in for releasing built-up stress on daily basis.

Workers who report high levels of stress spend nearly 50% more on healthcare each year compared to peers who are more-relaxed, according to a study published in the Journal of Occupational and Environmental Medicine.

Catey Hill, Wall Street Journal,
August 4, 2013

Today Cleveland Clinic offers wellness programs to employers and finds that physical issues – tobacco use, inactivity, poor nutrition – aren't the biggest problem. Rather, "stress support is our clients' No. 1 request," says Joe Sweet, an executive at Cleveland Clinic Wellness. "The workforce is experiencing increased stress, anxiety, and depression at all levels."

Geoff Colvin,
FORTUNE, August 11, 2014

Expand the definition of wellness

"...a state of complete physical, mental, and social well-being, and not merely the absence of disease or infirmity." - The World Health Organization.

Lasting Wellness starts inside out: Unleashes inner motivation by understanding the direct correlation between Wellness, Creativity and Career Success. Wellness is much more than just absence of disease. Wellness is celebration of life in its fullness – enjoying lasting health, a successful career and a fulfilling family/personal life.

Dis–ease: Not-at-Ease

The system/body not-at-ease, in conflict, out of balance, under stress, leading to psychosomatic illnesses (most of the doctor's office visits are for psychosomatic diseases)

Wellness: Leading a Healthy Lifestyle and Celebrating Life in its Fullness

Sickness is a disruption in the health-giving balance of the body; nutrition, personal habits, even thoughts and experiences were all believed by Hippocrates to be major health factors. In this thinking, it is not only the whole person who experiences illness; it is also the whole person who must be made well.

Sherwin B. Nuland, M.D.

Balance is the key to leading a healthy lifestyle

A healthy lifestyle leads to wellness

Wellness creates the MINT conditions for unleashing creativity and innovation

Creativity and innovation drive enterprise growth and career success

Exercise Makes You Smarter

Your brain has to work harder to solve problems when you're stressed. A study from Michigan State University finds. So be sure

to hit the gym before a packed workday to stay on your game.

SELF Magazine, October 2012

When we take time to exercise, relax and spend time with family, we're not shortchanging our career, but instead unleashing our natural creative potential by creating the required MINT conditions.

> Wellness is an active process of becoming aware and making choices leading to a healthy and fulfilling life.

"Taking self-time is ultimately one of the most unselfish things we can do. A woman taking care of herself will feel more confident, more attractive, more strong, and energized. And, she will have more to give."

Michelle Ritterman, M.D.

Health, creativity and happiness are the natural by-products of wellness - a healthy and balanced lifestyle celebrating life in its fullness.

Workers of every rank are told these days that wide-ranging curiosity and continuous learning are vital to thriving in the modern economy. Formal education matters, career counselors say, but real-life experience (celebrating life in its fullness) is often even more valuable.

Steve Jobs and the Rewards of Risk Taking, Steve Lohr, August 27, 2011, New York Times

Research has shown that balancing our beloved work with other interests enhances physical and mental well-being and actually increases productivity. And for those around us, it makes us much more interesting and desirable to know.

**Jim Blasingame,
Small Business Advocate**

Fred Smith, FedEx founder and CEO, has been recognized as one of the creative individuals in the U.S. Fred's life shows that it's possible to lead a growing enterprise, build a global icon and enjoy a balanced life. Bill Holstein, Chief Executive Magazine Editor-in-Chief, interviewed Fred and asked him, "How do you maintain work-life balance?" Fred replied, "I have a very great as you might imagine, full family life. I have grandchildren, I still have children in college, and I have some kids that are athletes. I love to go to their games and watch them, as I have for all of them. I play a lot of tennis; try to get my heart rate up."

Closing Thoughts

The last slide of my 'Enjoying Balance' workshops is a picture of a colorful hot air balloon, labeled 'LIFE'. Visualize that you and your loved ones are riding in this hot air balloon as it gently floats over beautiful landscapes – clear blue lakes, colorful hills, lush green valleys, roaring waterfalls, vibrant flower gardens, wild horses galloping on open meadows, a beautiful sunset, white sandy beaches lined with palm trees...

In the diagram below, the balloon is ready to take off but it is not able to. Why? The balloon is tied to a hook in the ground with a strong rope. Let us look at the letters that make up the word LIFE.

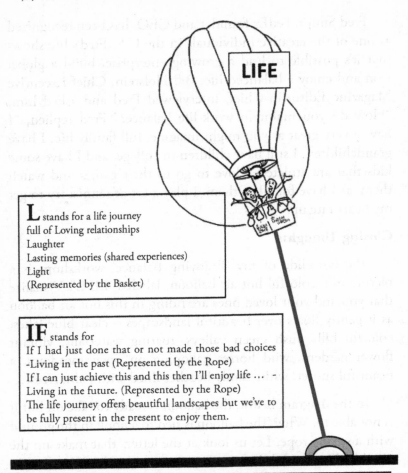

L stands for a life journey
full of Loving relationships
Laughter
Lasting memories (shared experiences)
Light
(Represented by the Basket)

IF stands for
If I had just done that or not made those bad choices
-Living in the past (Represented by the Rope)
If I can just achieve this and this then I'll enjoy life … -
Living in the future. (Represented by the Rope)
The life journey offers beautiful landscapes but we've to
be fully present in the present to enjoy them.

E stands for
Ego … My script is the right one. I've a script for your role also as to how you
should think and behave. 'You can only take off when I decide to release the
rope.' My needs come first. My ideas are the best. (Represented by hook in the
ground)
Life journey is much more enjoyable when we've people to share it with. The
deepest human need is 'I matter.' People in loving relationships understand and
respect each other's 'I matter needs,' scripts. Ego wants to control everything
and gets in the way of building and enjoying loving relationships.
I've personally experienced that controlling the ego is an ongoing process.

Enjoying the Balloon Ride (Life Journey) in the Age of Twitter

Three years ago I was at the office of John Wiley & Sons, publishers of my book, FedEx Delivers, to discuss the proposal for my next book. Matt Holt, Vice President and Executive Publisher, liked the idea and said, "Madan, this is the age of twitter. People don't have time to read. So, your next book must be half the size of FedEx Delivers. Your next book will be 25,000 words versus over 50,000 words in FedEx Delivers."

It's true that digital media has made it easier for everyone to keep up with world events and stay in touch with family and friends, but the constant feelings of 'being rushed' and what I call 'time poverty' negatively impact our attention span, not allowing us to linger on a web page for too long. Enjoying the balloon ride – a life full of loving relationships, shared experiences and laughter requires both – time, and a relaxed mind.

The habituation to simply skim the surface of experience, then move on, permeates our life. We don't know how to pause for contemplation, to take time for ourselves, to go from the frantic to the peaceful, to truly relax, to take note, to feel.

Stephan Rechtschaffen, M.D.,
Time Shifting: Creating Time to Enjoy Your Life,
Doubleday, 1996, New York

Yes, Life (and Time) Does Fly

After playing tennis regularly for a long time, I switched to golf a couple of years ago. The main reason for this switch was an opportunity to be outdoors and enjoy nature. Each golf course is different. The golf courses in Kauai, Hawaii and Torrey Pines in San Diego along the Pacific Ocean, both present unique landscapes. The challenge of learning a new sport was also very appealing to me.

I feel fortunate that at this stage in life, I've learnt not to worry too much about the score and just enjoy the shared experiences with friends in beautiful, natural settings. Having always been a competitive person by nature, I initially tended to pay too much attention to the score. A round of golf then became frustrating and stressful instead of being the relaxing outing it ought to have been. Yes, I do want to get better, that's why I head to the driving range whenever I can, and practice for hours on end.

The mild weather in Memphis allows us to play golf all year round. For the past year my golfing partner has been John, a successful school principal. We both prefer walking the course instead of riding a golf cart. In addition to getting some exercise while walking, we also get a chance to chat about our common interests, children, philosophies, sports and other things. We're at the same stage in our life journey - our children have grown up, moved out, and are working in other cities.

Last week, a young couple was playing ahead of us. John remarked, "Whenever I'm standing in the check-out line at the grocery store and see a young couple ahead of me with a baby in the stroller. I wish I could be young and do this all over again. I want to tell them, 'Enjoy the moment. They grow up fast! I miss my children who are working and living in other states.'"

We both wondered whether at that age we'd ever realized how fast time flies. We were busy moving up the professional ladder, taking on a mortgage, and dealing with myriad other life demands. Looking back, both of us felt grateful for the life we'd lived so far, especially that we were able to enjoy watching our kids growing up, and build lots of happy memories, the virtual V.I.D.E.O.s in the mind's hard drive.

For members of my family at least, these spring and summer hikes are a reminder that what shapes us is not so much the possessions we acquire but the memories we accumulate, that when you scrape away the veneer, what gives life meaning is not the grandest barbecue or the sportiest car. It's each other.

Sore, Happy Feet on the Pacific Trail
Nicholas Kristof, May 26, 2016, The New York Times

Trust me, one investment choice you'll be glad you made. A single flower (experience) by itself may seem insignificant but in sufficient number can color the hillside (life.)

Because everything is energy, including us, we're always contributing to the collective energy of the universe. When we're having fun, we send out the vibration of joy, uplifting the universal energy. So have some fun, and do it often! If need be, mark off time on your calendar with the word fun in order to make time for it.

We weren't created to be serious and inhibited, concerned about what others think, including the critic in our own mind. If you were raised to believe that fun was frivolous, you can let that old belief (script) go. Make a pact with yourself not to worry about what you think you should be doing – in this moment your job is to enjoy yourself.

Jane Beach, Science of Mind, April 2016

You were born to enjoy your life journey. Where do you begin? The answer is simple. Begin where you are right now! It does not matter what happened in the past. By reminding yourself that even God cannot change past, you can move past any setback or disappointment. Remember, this life is yours to live as you choose. Your future will be determined by the choices you make today.

Life journey is about learning and growing. Nature of all living things is to grow. Trees and other living things grow best when they exist in a balanced environment. Our growth as a human being is stifled when our lifestyle becomes unbalanced. The vitality, the inner energy stops renewing itself, and we feel restless and tired.

It's a beautiful life. Let us celebrate it in its fullness today, this week, this month, this year! With the busyness our lives get hijacked. We drift into a way of life and may not realize until it is too late that this is not the kind of life we wanted at all. You've the power to make life balance enhancing choices to experience the joy, serenity, vitality and creativity that you deserve.

> A well-lived life is not some grand achievement but how you experience joy in life's simple pleasures every week. Forget your portfolio this week. Invest time in shared experiences.

Enjoy lifetoday and build memories! It's later than you think.

A successful and well-lived life is when you look back and the memories (V.I.D.E.O.s in the mind's hard drive) make you smile.

❑ ❑ ❑

Author

Author (left) presenting a copy of
his first book on this subject,
'Best of Both Worlds: Career and Marriage' to Fred
Smith, Founder and CEO of FedEx

Madan Birla, both for personal and professional reasons,
has been passionately interested and active in the work/life
balance field for a long time.

He was born and grew up in New Delhi. After completing high schooling in New Delhi, he did his undergraduate work in Mechanical Engineering at the Birla Institute of Technology and Science (BITS) in Pilani. Following that he enrolled at the Illinois Institute of Technology (IIT) in Chicago, IL, where he received his Master of Science degree in Industrial Engineering. After graduating from IIT, he joined RCA Records in Indianapolis. While in Indianapolis he did graduate work in Business at Butler University. After moving to Memphis to join FedEx, he received a Master of Science degree in Counseling from the University of Memphis.

He is a veteran of the "hard" side of business. In his 22 years at FedEx, he was Managing Director of Long-Range Planning before being named Managing Director in the company's Leadership Institute. For eight years as a member of the Long Range Planning Committee he worked closely with Fred Smith and the senior management team in evaluating strategic 'what-ifs'. At the FedEx Leadership Institute, he excelled as a facilitator of Innovation, Leadership and Life Balance courses for all levels of management throughout the world. For the last ten years he has been advising executives on how to unleash employee creativity and commitment to build a culture of innovation and performance.

During his annual trips to India he speaks to students and executives at IIM-Bangalore, IIM-Kolkata, ISB, IIT-Madras, BITS-Pilani and other universities. He is a regular speaker at professional and business group meetings in the U.S. including Society of Human Resource Management (SHRM) Global Human Resource Forums in New York and Monterey, CA, Alliance of Work/Life Professionals, annual conference in New Orleans, American Management Association, Executive Forums in New York, Chicago, and San Francisco, Tennessee

Leadership conference and Leadership Academy, Illinois Institute of Technology, Chicago, IL.

He has received many awards including Membership in Alpha-Pi-Mu, Industrial Engineering Honor Society, Honorary Citizen, City of Indianapolis for community involvement, inducted into College of Education Alumni Hall of Fame at the University of Memphis and Five-Star Awards, the highest recognition for Leadership Excellence at FedEx.

He is actively involved in volunteer work for giving back to the community. He led the effort to establish the Indian Community Fund for Greater Memphis that funded the permanent exhibits including the Gandhi exhibit at the National Civil Rights Museum in Memphis and 'Windows to the World' an interactive educational exhibit at the Children's Museum of Memphis. He developed long range plans for the Church Health Center (serving working poor), Friends for Life (serving HIV/AIDS affected population), and the Tipton County Commission on Aging (serving seniors). He lives with his wife Shashi in Collierville, TN and has two grown children who live in New York and Chicago.

Yes, it's possible to enjoy both, a successful career and a fulfilling personal/family life

Author (Left) receiving his second five star award, the highest recognition for leadership excellence at FedEx from Fred Smith, founder and CEO of FedEx

Co-author

Co-author, Dr. Cecilia Miller Marshall, Ph.D., is a licensed psychologist in private practice in Oxford, Mississippi. Educated at Rhodes College, the University of Louisville, and the University of Mississippi, she has 20 years' experience in individual and family counseling. Her family includes her husband, two daughters, a dog and two horses.

❏ ❏ ❏

Other books by Madan Birla

"As Dean at a business school that has made innovation a key element of our culture, it is fascinating to read Madan Birla's account of how FedEx instilled that value for competitive advantage. His insights into the entire journey involved in innovation – and the organizational design it requires – make FedEx Delivers required reading for students and managers alike."

- Dipak Jain, Dean, Kellogg School of Management, Northwestern University.....

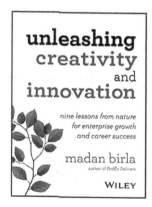

"Madan is a great storyteller who offers simple practical and very actionable insights in Unleashing Creativity and Innovation. Very impressive."

-Sanjay Khosla, former President, Kraft Foods, Inc.

For more information please visit
www.madanbirla.com

The author's proceeds from the book will be donated to Educate Girls, a nonprofit organization that is holistically tackling issues at the root cause of gender inequality in India's education system.

About Educate Girls

Educate Girls works in around 12,000+ schools across 8,000+ villages in Ajmer, Bhilwara, Bundi, Jalore, Jhalawar, Pali, Rajsamand, Sirohi and Udaipur districts of Rajasthan and Jhabua district of Madhya Pradesh, India.

VISION

Educate Girls aims to achieve behavioural, social and economic transformation for all girls towards an India where all children have equal opportunities to access quality education.

MISSION

Educate Girls leverages existing community and government resources to ensure that all girls are in school and learning well.

GOAL

Educate Girls aims to improve access and quality of education for around 2.8 Million marginalized and under served children. By 2018, Educate Girls will reach out to over 27,000 schools across 16 districts in India.

For more information please visit www.educategirls.ngo